TRANSFORMATION

When the worst of her tears were over, Sheila rose and walked across her room to her dresser and the mask.

She touched it and felt a slight, electric shock. It was a strange vibration, as if it were charged with the magic of infinite dreams and possibilities. The mask was more beautiful than she had remembered. The face plate was made of a strange white lace so fine that it was almost transparent.

She thought of all the horrible things her parents had said to one another and wished desperately for some way to escape. The mask tingled even more violently. She raised it to her face, wondering if she would even be able to see out of it. She pulled on the silk string and slipped it over her head. Suddenly, she felt the surface of the mask press against her bare flesh with startling speed. The ferocity of the pressure felt like a thousand needles coming to life.

Without warning, a fiery hand reached into her brain. Colors exploded before her eyes. She wanted to scream, she wanted to get help, but it was too late. The world vanished into blackness.

When she finally awakened, she rose and looked in the mirror. Fear coursed through her.

"It can't be," she whispered. "It can't!"

The girl staring back from the mirror was beautiful—but she was no longer Sheila.

NOW OPEN!
THE NIGHT OWL CLUB

Pool Tables, Video Games, Great Munchies,
Dance Floor, Juke Box, *Live* Bands On Weekend.

* * *

Bring A Date Or Come Alone . . .

* * *

Students From Cooper High School,
Hudson Military Academy,
Cooper Riding Academy for Girls
Especially Welcome . . .

* * *

Located Just Outside Of Town.
Take Thirteen Bends Road,
Or Follow Path Through Woods.

* * *

Don't Let The Dark Scare You Away . . .

* * *

Jake and Jenny Demos-proprietors
Teen club, no alcohol served.

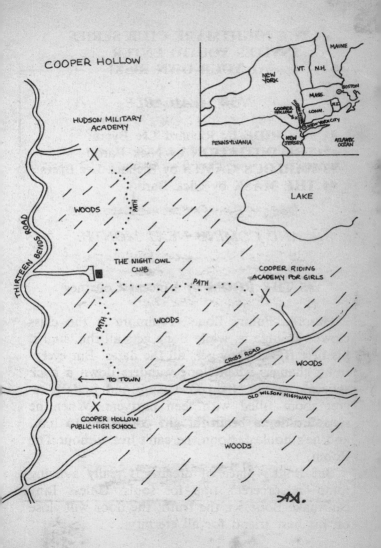

#4: THE MASK

Nick Baron

Z·FAVE
KENSINGTON PUBLISHING CORP.

To my beloved Denise

One

Sheila Holland felt the soft caress of sunlight as it broke through the steel gray clouds, through the window of her fifth period Natural Studies class, and touched the side of her face. Sitting at her desk, she closed her eyes and pretended that the sunlight was the strong, warm hand of Ian Montgomery touching her. Pretending was all she could do. Ian didn't know she was alive, and he probably never would.

The light faded. Sheila opened her eyes and shifted her gaze to the clock on the other side of the classroom. Eleven fifty-five. Ten more minutes and Mrs. Lang's class would be over. Twenty-five of her classmates surrounded her. Sheila knew the names of each student. She had gone to school with many of them since childhood. Their names were the most intimate detail any of them had personally revealed to her in all the years she had known them. It had been long before this, her junior year, that Sheila had given up on learning anything but second-hand knowl-

9

edge of her schoolmates. She was different from them, and they would never let her forget it.

Her teacher, a startlingly attractive raven-haired woman, stood at the front of the class delivering a lecture. Sheila liked Mrs. Lang. When she first saw the woman, she had been prepared to hate her. Erika Lang was five-foot-six, trim, soft, and beautiful. Her features were dark and mysterious. The woman's midnight hair spilled onto milk white shoulders that led to a magnificent, hourglass figure and long, perfect legs.

Sheila knew that she possessed no such attributes. She wasn't deformed or anything, she was simply *underdeveloped*. Or so she felt whenever she looked in the mirror. Sheila was five-foot-one, in shape, but lacking any real figure, and cursed to look like a thirteen-year-old even though she was now a junior in high school.

She had brown, wavy hair that dropped to her narrow shoulders; sad, brown, milk-carton-kid's eyes; and a nose that was a little too round and wide for her narrow, oval face and thin lips. She hid her slightly large ears under her hair whenever possible. Today, she wore jeans, a sweater, and a silver love bracelet one of her second cousins gave her as a joke. But she treasured the item because she was the only one who knew that it had not come from her imaginary "out-of-town boyfriend." Sheila had never had a boyfriend. Lots of male friends, but no one that was interested in her romantically.

She wished one boy was interested in her, though—one special boy. Ian Montgomery was Cooper Hollow's answer to Tom Cruise. Sheila was about to drop back into another fantasy about life with Ian when she suddenly heard Mrs. Lang calling her name. She looked up abruptly and knew she must have looked like a deer caught in a car's headlights. The other students burst out laughing.

"Sheila, so good of you to join us," Mrs. Lang teased.

She smiled weakly. "Sorry."

In the back of the classroom, a student made a crack. "Yeah, we are, too," it sounded like. Followed by more snickering and laughing.

"We're talking about political repression. Countries suppressing the rights of their people and denying them simple human dignities. Prisoners of conscience. Men and women beaten, tortured, starved, even killed due to their beliefs. I thought you might have something to add."

"Here comes Ms. Brainiac," someone else whispered. "Computing, computing . . ."

More laughter, only a bit restrained.

Fear twisted and gnashed within Sheila's guts. "Sounds like a typical day at Cooper High."

That met with more laughter, but this time, it was the right kind. The kids were laughing *with* her, not *at* her. Sheila knew it wouldn't last. Nevertheless, she smiled nervously and sank a little in her chair, enjoying the moment. Mrs. Lang exhaled a ragged breath, obviously disappointed, and turned sharply to call upon another student.

As class wore on, Sheila found that she had mixed feelings about the remark she had made. No further derisive comments were launched in her direction, and for that, she was grateful. But Mrs. Lang gave her several sidelong glances that told Sheila the woman was less than pleased.

Finally, the bell rang. Sheila gathered up her books and was ready to bolt for the rear exit when her teacher called her.

"I'd like to see you for a moment, please," said Mrs. Lang.

The laughter returned with ooohs and ahhhs. "The brain is gonna get hers. That would be a first."

The classroom cleared quickly. Sheila made one more attempt to escape, "I'm gonna be late for class."

"This'll only take a minute. I'll give you a pass."

Sheila hung her shoulders in defeat, picked up her books, and walked to Mrs. Lang's desk. Her teacher was wearing a white silk top and a black skirt. The skirt ended just above the knees and had a small slit on the side. The woman sat on the edge of the desk, her long, perfect legs crossed.

Sheila would kill to look like this woman. She wondered if Mrs. Lang was even half aware of the effect she had on the teenaged boys she taught. Sheila often heard the boys at lunch, in the halls, and at the Night Owl Club. Their comments were sometimes crude, sometimes dreamy, but always attentive. Yes, Sheila would kill for that kind of notice. Instead, she was just a brainy little geek who looked more like a thirteen-year-old boy than a knockout like Mrs. Lang.

"What happened?" Mrs. Lang asked.

"I don't know."

"Is it my imagination or did we have an hour long talk after school on Monday about both of us being members of Freedom International and what the organization meant to us?"

"No," Sheila said, suddenly ashamed. "You didn't imagine it."

"Were you nervous?"

Sheila bit her lip. That explanation was as good as any, but she didn't want to lie. "No, I wasn't."

"This could have been a real opportunity for you to show what you've learned."

"You did a good enough job. You didn't need me."

"I can hand out the facts. But I know from talking to you the other day that Freedom International and all it is trying to accomplish is very important to you. You said it yourself, the organization needs the support of younger members. Reaching kids with views that are still developing is best accomplished by the testimony of other

13

kids, not with speeches made by adults."

Sheila became angry. "I do my part, all right?"

"Yes," Mrs. Lang said, her voice becoming impossibly softer and even more compassionate. "Of course. I wasn't trying to beat up on you. I just want to understand. Are you worried about others knowing that you're in Freedom?"

"No."

Mrs. Lang shook her head. "It seems like you're ashamed of your intelligence and your knowledge. You shouldn't be. Those assets are so important—"

"Didn't you hear what they said? I'm the geek, I'm the brain. I have all the answers. I'm not like them."

"And you want to be?"

Sheila bit her lip. She looked back to the doorway to make sure no one had come in for the next class. In a small, strangled voice she said, "You don't know what it's like. Just once I'd like to be asked out on a date or invited to a party. Just once. They're doing a three night masquerade at the Night Owl Club. It starts tonight, it ends Friday. Halloween."

Mrs. Lang's face lit up. "That's *wonderful*. Why don't you go, you'll have a wonderful time."

"Yeah, right. I'm just going to show up there? Alone? No one's invited me. As long as people see me as this geeky brain and nothing else, I don't have a chance."

"You can't worry about what other people

14

think about you," Mrs. Lang said. "Sheila, you're going to look back on these years and realize that what ultimately matters is how you see yourself. Be true to yourself."

"That's easy for you to say. You're pretty."

"You're pretty, too, Sheila."

"Then why am I always alone?" Sheila asked as she turned and ran from the classroom.

Two

Ian Montgomery, number seventy-one, commanded the football field. When he was loosed, he was like a Juggernaut — no one could stop him. The few that managed to lay hands on him were soon face down on the ground. The rest found themselves gripping thin air as he raced across the playing field, leaving his competition hopelessly in the dust.

Sheila's camera followed his every movement. Her lens trained on him with unerring precision. The feelings he elicited within her, however, were anything but cool and detached. She thought he was magnificent. In all her life, she had never seen anything quite like him. She never missed seeing him play, even when, like today, it was only a practice session.

Suddenly a nightmarish shape crowded into her line of vision. Sheila saw crossed hazel eyes, dark unkempt hair, and a squashed button nose. The girl staring into her camera pulled back her lips to make herself look bucktoothed.

"I said, communist pinko marshmallow eaters from the Gamma Quadrant just took over the White House. They've held their first news conference. In it, they stated that by the time Sheila Holland is twenty-five, her boobs will be somewhere around her ankles."

"Thirty," Sheila said, easing her camera from her face and staring into the sardonic visage of her best friend, Gwen Turko. Gwen was a junior, like Sheila, and she dressed in blue jeans, a denim jacket, and a Mickey Mouse tee-shirt pulled down over her waist. Her sunglasses were jammed high into the curly mass that constituted her hair. She had never grown out of the tomboy stage.

"Huh?"

"I've seen pictures of my mom. I'd give it 'til I'm thirty, then it all goes to hell. If I *had* any boobs, that is. Which I don't."

"It's nice to know you're paying attention," Gwen said in her usual sarcastic manner.

They stood on a set of bleachers far enough from the coach and the other players to ensure their comfort and privacy, but close enough to the field to get fantastic shots. Sheila and Gwen were members of the photography club and Nikons hung from both their necks.

"What were you, off in Monkey-Boy dreamland again?" Gwen asked.

"Monkey-Boy" was Gwen's term for Ian. Sheila didn't like it much, but she said nothing. Gwen

17

couldn't understand Sheila's continuing obsession with Ian. She had never been out on a date and had no interest in having a boyfriend. The concept of loving someone the way Sheila loved Ian—even though he didn't know it—was alien to her.

" 'Fraid so."

On the playing field, the coach called for the athletes to gather, and the animal ferocity seemed to suddenly drain out of Ian Montgomery. He walked back to the coach with an ease and confidence that allowed his movements to be categorized just this side of a strut. Several onlookers called his number. He looked up at them, smiled, and waved.

"Turbo!" one of the players shouted. "When are you gonna get a man?"

"Why? You know where I can find one, meatball?" Gwen shouted in return. When she spoke again, it was only to Sheila. "Mark again. God, I really want to kick his butt."

Sheila nodded. Gwen's last name was Turko, but her friends and detractors alike sometimes called her Turbo, instead. She was always *on* about something, ready to go into battle for any cause. If none existed, she was prepared to make one up.

Her relatives, teachers, and family physician warned that she would suffer either a heart attack, an ulcer, a cerebral hemorrhage, or all of them if she didn't slow down. Gwen told them to take a chill and relax. She'd live to be one hundred and six and dance on their graves.

Her habit of making gruesome statements like that had led her—at her parents' insistence—into one long conference with the school psychiatrist. The result had been an interchange between the doctor and Gwen about who had a more extensive library of useless facts about horror movies, herself or the counselor. The psychiatrist, named Carrie White, had grown up sharing a name with one of Stephen King's most popular creations. Her sympathies were with Gwen.

In the most polite, scholarly terms, Dr. White told Gwen's parents to take a chill. Their daughter would easily live to be one hundred and six and would, most assuredly, take great delight in dancing on a *lot* of people's graves. She was too healthy, both in mind and body, and too ornery, for any other fate.

On the field, Mark Phillips, player sixty-nine, made a kissy-motion to Gwen and went to the huddle with his buddies. His walk could *only* be catalogued as a strut.

A few weeks ago, at another practice, Mark had aimed his butt at the girls and told them to get a real good shot. Gwen was obliging. A friend of hers on the school newspaper had been all set to run the shot with the byline, "Mark Phillips Displays His Private Assets." The faculty advisor, a close friend of the coach, pulled it. Sheila's photos occasionally made the newspaper.

19

Not coincidentally, they were always of Ian.

"Have you ever wondered what it would be like to be down there?" Sheila asked, her gaze drifting to the players who were conversing with their coach as several cheerleaders looked on. "Wouldn't it be nice, just once, to be on the inside, looking out, instead of the other way around?"

"Don't be a *pod*," Gwen said, referring to the aliens in the film "Invasion of the Body Snatchers."

"I'm not a pod," Sheila said with a touch of resentment.

Gwen shook her head. "Sure, I've wondered. I've also wondered what it would be like to be awake without an anesthetic during open heart surgery. Doesn't mean I want to experience it."

Sheila felt her anger rise. "Don't you take anything seriously?"

"Okay, I'll tell you exactly what it would be like." Suddenly, Gwen assumed an exaggerated upper New York preppy overbite and said, " 'Hi, Buffy.'

" 'Oh, hi, Biff.'

" 'How was football practice?'

" 'Oh, fine, but would you *please* be careful about how much starch you put in my shorts? They seem to be riding up at the most inopportune times.'

" 'Yes, dear. Of course, dear. Anything you *say*, dear. Oh, darling, would you like me to lay

20

down so you can walk all over me with your cleats on?'

" 'Oh, would you?' "

"Thanks a lot," Sheila said coldly. She had spent the last half hour before Gwen's arrival fantasizing about what life would be like if Ian Montgomery loved her. The last thing she needed was having her secret dream ridiculed.

"Hey, I was just kidding," Gwen said, her tone softening uncharacteristically. Sheila's stonelike expression did not change. "I was just *kidding,* lighten up."

"Okay," Sheila said impassively. "Whatever."

"You know how I feel about those people—"

"I know. You hate them, they hate you. You're even."

Gwen was surprised by the sharpness of her friend's tone. "I'm not saying you're wrong, but you can really be pretty cold sometimes, you know?"

"She's got it bad, what do you want?" a boy said from somewhere close. The sound of his voice made both girls jump. They turned and saw Jack Kidder standing behind them.

Three

Jack had climbed onto the bleachers behind them without making a sound. He was tall and skinny, with a long, thin face, wild eyes, and a scarecrow's uneven smile. His dark hair constantly flopped into his eyes. Using his elongated, pianist's hands, Jack brushed it away. He wore an army jacket that had once belonged to his dad, who was now in prison. A backpack was slung over his shoulders.

"Don't do that," Gwen and Sheila said in unison.

"Do what?" Jack asked as he stepped down to their row and sat between them.

"Sneak up on us like that," Gwen said as she slugged him in the arm hard enough to make him yelp with pain. The camera he wore around his neck slapped against his chest.

"All right, all right," he said. Then he gave Sheila a goofy grin. "I guess that's the most physical contact I can expect from my little love poodle today."

"I guess so."

Gwen moaned. Jack was always calling her ridiculous pet names. "I'd hit you again, but I'm worried you might like it too much."

"Only one way to find out."

Gwen slammed him in the same spot. From his cry of pain and surprise, he evidently did not like it at all.

Rubbing his sore arm, Jack said, "I've got everything cleared for us at the Wakefield Mall."

Her eyes flashing open wide, Gwen said, "You're kidding, right?"

Jack shook his head.

"That's great," Sheila said distractedly. Ian was taking the field once again and she raised her camera to follow his movements.

"The Wakefield Mall," Gwen said, getting ready to punch Jack again. "All right!"

Jack sprang out of the way just in time. "You really need to learn some other way of expressing yourself."

Gwen shrugged.

"I thought they were worried about the controversy," Sheila said as she watched Ian intently and snapped another picture of him.

"New guy took over. He's a member of Freedom International, too. He said we can set up a booth there and distribute flyers all we want. Just try to be cool about it. Don't wrestle anyone to the ground to get them to listen, and be polite if we get any real jerks."

"All right," Gwen said again. Wakefield was in the next county, but the large two-story mall was always crowded.

Jack pulled a sketchbook from his backpack and flipped it open to a certain page. "I thought we could go with 'Wake up, Wakefield!' as our slogan. I printed this out on the laser printer in the computer room. What do you think?"

Gwen nodded. Sheila was lost in the viewfinder once more. Gwen tapped Sheila's butt with the tip of her sneaker. Spinning around, startled, Sheila quickly realized what was going on and said the slogan looked great. "Very attention-getting."

Jack nodded. "People are dying, people are having their civil liberties denied to them; we've got to do our part."

"Absolutely—" Sheila began. Someone cried touchdown, and she whirled back to the playing field and cursed. Ian had scored a goal, and she had missed it.

"They want us there on Thursday to set up," Jack said. "Does that work for you two?"

"Yeah," Gwen said.

Sheila felt embarrassed at paying so little attention to her friends. This was a lot more important than staring at Ian, she told herself. If only she could bring herself to believe that. "Absolutely."

"You're not going to run off to the masquerade, are you?" Jack said, teasing.

Sheila sighed. I wish, she wanted to say, but she kept her mouth shut. Ian would be there. Her thoughts suddenly snapped back to the weekend. She had gone to an antique barn with her mother on Sunday. They had spent nearly an hour without finding anything before Sheila came upon the mask.

It was the most beautiful thing she had ever seen, other than Ian Montgomery. She took one look at it and knew she had to own it, even though she would probably have no real use for it. Under other circumstances, her mother might have objected to her throwing away her meager allowance on such an extravagance, but Colleen Holland had other things on her mind. She and Sheila's dad, Gary, had gone through another of their knockdown fights, and Colleen had simply wanted to be out of the house.

Fantasies of going to the masquerade and approaching Ian wearing the mask flashed into Sheila's mind. Maybe she could trick him into loving her. He could get to know her with the mask on, and she would be beautiful because of it, then —

Stupid, she chided herself. Stupid, stupid, stupid. No mask could give her what she needed to compete with the senior girls and the cheerleaders. She would need a miracle for that.

"The only possible conflict I can see is the deadline for the photography contest," Jack said as he tapped his camera. "They want all the entries in by Monday."

Sheila nodded. The *Cooper Hollow Gazette* sponsored the contest every year. The winner's work was displayed in a gallery downtown and published in the paper's weekend edition.

Jack checked his watch. "I gotta go. Melissa's meeting me at four."

Gwen raised one eyebrow. "Melissa Antonelli?"

"Uh-huh."

Melissa was one of the prettiest girls in the senior class. Jack had had a crush on her for years.

Gwen knocked lightly on the side of Jack's head. "Hey! Hey, you! Anyone in there? Don't you remember the last time you shot your mouth off that someone like her was dating you? Her boyfriend beat the hell out of you."

Jack shook his head. "I didn't say we were going out. She's modeling for me. We're going down to the graveyard. There're some really great photo ops there. I figure I'll do some grainy black and white double exposures. She's going to wear this old frilly dress that belonged to her great, great grandmother or something like that. It'll be fun."

Sheila understood now. Melissa wanted to be a model one day. Posing for Jack would give her something to show the agencies. She hoped Jack realized that's all it was and not get his hopes up. Melissa usually hung around with creeps like Mark Phillips, not decent guys like Jack.

From Jack's goofy, glazed expression, she could tell that he had concocted an entire scenario in his head. If she said anything, he would just get defensive.

"Who knows, maybe I'll even get some good portfolio stuff out of it. Something to show a good school—like Cooper Union, or Visual Arts."

Sheila smiled. Jack wanted to be a professional photographer in the worst way.

"Let's meet at lunch tomorrow and we'll set everything up for Wakefield," he said excitedly.

"Sounds good, Jack," Sheila said, wanting desperately to say something to him, knowing the whole time that it would cause more harm than good. He packed up and ran off.

"She's going to break his heart," Sheila said.

Gwen nodded slowly. "If she does, I'll kill her."

"I'll help."

This time, they both attempted to lose themselves in the practice. Suddenly, Gwen asked, "You're really thinking of going tonight, aren't you?"

"What do you mean?"

"The masquerade."

"I dunno."

"I'll go with you, if you want."

"I don't think either of us would really fit in there, do you?"

"Hey, I'll go anywhere I like. No one's going to tell me where I can and can't go."

"No, they don't *tell* you, they just make sure you wish you were anyplace else, that's all."

"You're right, who needs them, anyway?"

I do, Sheila thought as she watched Ian on the playing field. More than I can tell you.

They watched the rest of the practice in silence.

28

Four

Two weeks earlier, in Mrs. Lang's class, Sheila had seen a reference to Dante's *Inferno*. She found the text in the library and flipped through the illustrations of the various levels of hell envisioned by the artist. Sitting in silence at the dinner table with her mother and father as they glared at one another, Sheila started to wonder if there had been a few levels that Dante had left out. If so, living with angry parents had to be one of them.

For days, Sheila had wished that her parents would stop arguing. But the brooding silence that had taken the place of the shouting and fiery accusations was even more difficult to handle. Their dinner consisted of leftover barbecue chicken, frozen vegetables, and a tossed salad. The lettuce leaves were turning brown. Sheila considered mentioning this to her mother, but one ice cold glance from the woman was enough to tell her to keep her mouth closed. She helped set the table, mentioned the awareness booster she would be participating in for Freedom International over the weekend, and generally did her best to avoid any subjects that might set the woman off.

She was lucky in one aspect. Her mom and dad did not take their anger out on her, like Gwen's parents. Gwen's mother found fault with everything her daughter did. The woman had an unnerving habit of stopping Gwen just before she left for school to tell her that they had to "have a discussion" that night. Gwen said it didn't bother her, but Sheila could see the tension mounting in her friend as the day went on.

At night, with her stomach in knots, Gwen would prepare for a battle over some infinitesimal infraction that she had committed against her mother's fluctuating set of rules to live by. Then the "discussion" would only be a letter that had come for her. Something harmless like that. When real trouble was on the way, Gwen would get no warning. One minute, everything would be fine, the next, she was the daughter who had let her parents down; a terrible child, a mistake, a willful, ungrateful little brat who didn't deserve anything her parents had slaved to give her.

Sheila had been waiting for the day to arrive when her mother and father started doing the same thing to her, but, so far, she had been spared that kind of abuse.

I'm dancing as fast as I can, Lord, Sheila thought as they said grace. *I'm dancing as fast as*

I can.

Dinner went on. There was one light momen.
when Colleen talked about a scene in a sitcom
from the other night. But the laughter faded
quickly, and the tension immediately returned.

Colleen was forty-one, and the years had taken
their toll on her youthful beauty. Crow's feet
gathered in the corners of her eyes, deep smile
lines marked her face, and the muscles of her
neck had turned wiry. Her skin, once luminous—
if Sheila could believe old photographs—was now
dried out. She had dark blue eyes, short hair, and
a figure that had once been stunning, and was
now shot. The hourglass had become an accor-
dion, or so she had told Sheila. She wore gray
sweats and walked around barefoot.

Her father, Gary, had lost much of his blond
hair, and had resorted to allowing it to grow long
so that he could flop it over on one side to cover
his baldness. His face was sturdy, and might have
been considered handsome, if it was not-so-thor-
oughly average. His jacket had been draped on
the back of his chair and his red "power tie"
hung loosely around his neck, slicing into the
field of his crisp white shirt like a blood stain.

Soon the meal was finished and Sheila offered
to clear. She saw the way her parents were staring
at each other and wanted to be as far away as
possible when the argument erupted. As it turned
out, she was in the kitchen, washing off the
dishes, when the angry screams began. Sheila put

31

down the plate she had been holding and went to the barroom-style slatted double doors. She peeked through one corner and saw her parents gesturing wildly with their hands.

"You don't *know* that," Gary hollered.

"Fine, I don't know anything, do I? You're the smart one. You're the one with all the answers. I'm just the bimbo who fell in love with you and gave up her dreams so that you could go after yours. Not that anything I've done counts for anything."

"We are seventy-one *thousand* dollars in debt, Colleen. I didn't see you complaining every time we went out to a fancy restaurant. I didn't hear you telling me not to buy all that crap you said we needed over the years. All the clothes, all the furniture—"

"Yeah, right, I'm at fault for wanting to feed and clothe our family. We should have gone naked and eaten crumbs off the floor. Gimme a break. Like I'm the one who had to have the Porsche that was in the shop twice a week for five years. I'm the one who had to buy at least two of every new stereo component, VCR, and whatever-the-hell-else just because it was there. I'm the one that if something broke, instead of trying to fix it, I'd pile it in the corner and buy a new one, then lose the receipt so that we couldn't get it serviced, even if we wanted to.

"You're right, Gary. That's the important stuff. Those are the essentials. Hell, we could have just

32

gotten rid of the house and lived in the Porsche, couldn't we? I mean, that's the way to create a stable home environment for our daughter, right?"

Standing at the door, Sheila suddenly felt her stomach muscles tighten.

"Don't bring her into this," Gary said. "This isn't about her."

"No? Well, maybe it should be. Don't you see what this is doing to her? Her grades are slipping. She's getting dark circles under her eyes because she's not sleeping right any more. She spends as little time as possible in this house and I'll tell you, Gary, I don't blame her. I don't blame her one bit."

"Yeah? So what are you saying?"

"I'm not *saying* anything. It's just that we're not going to have the money to put her through college like we promised. Or did you forget that we tapped her college fund last summer just to keep the household going? You said it was just until you got a better job. Just until things turned around and really got going for you, that's what you said."

"So what am I supposed to do? Haven't you seen the news? The economy's in the toilet. We're lucky we have jobs at all," yelled Sheila's father.

"Yeah, sure. This is exactly what I wanted to do with my B.A. in business administration. Clean offices in the middle of the night. Water plants during the day."

"The firm is talking about expanding, about opening an office in the city. Advertising's a tough field, but I've managed to stay in it for twenty years. That counts for something. If the New York office happens, I've been told I'm first in line to head it up."

"Yeah, right. How many times have we heard that? Every time you're up for a promotion, they give it some new guy, some fresh guy, some *young* guy—"

"Thanks, Colleen, thanks for reminding me. What would I do without your loving support?"

"I'm just saying that right now, if we were a real two income family, maybe we wouldn't be in this kind of trouble. If I could have finished graduate school instead of taking work as a secretary—"

"Hey, you could have gone back to school at any time. No one was stopping you."

"Right. And who was going to raise Sheila? You? What a joke. You can't even take care of yourself. I'm telling you, Gary, things are going to have to level out. I'm really tired of living on this roller coaster."

"So what do you want me to do, huh? What is it you want? You want to stop the ride and get off?"

"Maybe that's not such a bad idea."

"Anytime."

"Yeah, right. Look, just leave me alone, all right? I don't want to deal with this any more tonight. Just leave me alone so I can try and think. It would be so nice just to have some peace and quiet so I could *think* for a change."

Sheila watched as they stared at one another. Her father broke the silence, "I'm going out."

"Fine," Colleen said. "You do that."

Sheila turned away from the door and went back to the dishes. Somehow, she had to keep herself from crying. She couldn't let her mother know that she was listening.

Colleen came in. "Why don't you go on, honey. I'll finish up here. I need something to do."

Sheila nodded, afraid to speak, terrified that if she tried, she would end up in her own shouting match with her mother. Instead, she wiped her hands and hurriedly left the kitchen. She went upstairs, to her bedroom, and locked the door behind her. Sliding down the back of the door, her hands covering her face, she allowed herself the luxury of tears. Deep, wrenching sobs were called forth so forcefully that they caused the agony of the soul with which she had become all too familiar to surface again.

She didn't want to be here. She didn't want this to be her life. Though she loved both her parents, she didn't know how much more of this she could take.

Finally, when the worst of her tears had been torn from her, Sheila rose, walked to her dresser, and yanked a handful of tissues from the dispenser. Sitting beside the tissue holder was the glorious prize she had bought over the weekend. Sheila blew her nose, took some more tissues to wipe away the tears, then picked up the mask.

When she touched it, she felt a slight, electric shock, a strange vibration, as if it were charged with the magic of infinite dreams and possibilities. The mask was more beautiful than she had remembered. The face plate was made of a strange white lace so fine that it was almost transparent. The material alone shouldn't have been strong enough to hold the molded features of a startlingly beautiful woman, but the fabric had been treated with some substance that held it in shape.

Upon the face plate lay fantastic designs of midnight blue, emerald green, sparkling gold, and bloody crimson. They spiraled and danced upon the surface of the mask as Sheila turned it this way and that, fascinated by the trick of light that made the designs appear to shift and metamorphose. Strands of fabric created laser thin feathers that reached out from the eyebrows, and the crown of the mask, meant for holding a long, lustrous mane of hair, was a strange yet lovely design that might have come from ancient Egypt or some mysterious, forgotten culture. At its center lay an upside-down cross with a loop on the bottom and surrounding that were several tiers of ghostlike figures straining heavenward, reaching for an altar made of swords. Sheila wondered what the inverted cross symbolized.

She thought of all the horrible things her parents had said to one another and wished desperately for some way to escape. The mask tingled even more violently. She raised it to her face, wondering if she would even be able to see out of it, and pulled the silk cord out so that she could slip it over her head. The surface of the mask pressed against her bare flesh with startling speed. The ferocity of the pressure felt like a thousand needles suddenly coming to life.

Without warning, a fiery hand reached into her brain. Colors exploded before her eyes. She wanted to scream, she wanted to get help, but it was too late.

The world suddenly vanished and darkness became her entire existence.

Five

Sheila had blacked out. She found herself lying on the floor, her bare flesh tingling.

Bare flesh?

Tentatively, Sheila ran her fingers over her naked skin. She turned her head and saw her clothing next to her on the floor in a heap. Sitting up slowly, she picked through her clothes and saw that they had been torn to shreds, ripped apart as if razor-sharp talons had sliced through them.

Had she done this? She didn't remember. Fear suddenly coursed through her. She had suffered some kind of seizure. That was the only explanation. A psychotic episode in which she had torn her clothes off and hacked them up.

Right. She had done all that, but she had been quiet enough not to alarm her mother, who was still downstairs. It had been a polite psychotic episode. A kinder, gentler seizure.

All right, that doesn't work. She had to find another explanation.

The fear returned as another possibility presented itself. Someone had attacked her. She had not been alone in her room after all.

Sheila leaped to her feet, anxious to study herself in the mirror over her dresser. If someone had attacked her, she would be covered in welts.

The girl staring back from the mirror was not Sheila. For a moment, Sheila couldn't breathe. She closed her eyes and tried to calm herself. In health, they had been taught relaxation techniques. Long, slow deep breaths. Hold them, then release.

Sheila opened her eyes. The face in the mirror, that of the stranger, had not changed.

What the hell was going on here?

Turning from the mirror before her legs gave out, Sheila crumpled upon the bed and drew herself up in a fetal position. This was a dream. It had to be. There was no other explanation.

Why couldn't she wake up?

Attempting once again to apply relaxation techniques, Sheila lay flat on the bed, tensed her entire body, then slowly allowed herself to relax, starting with her toes, then gradually traveling up to her head. It helped a little. She repeated this move several times, then became aware of something tickling the sides of her face. Long, lustrous, midnight black hair. With trembling fingers, she reached up and touched the silky strands.

It just can't be real, it can't!

Sheila sat bolt upright, then turned and looked

once more in the mirror. The stranger's expression revealed that she was just as frightened as Sheila. Shaking, Sheila touched the generous expanse of wild black hair that wreathed her face. In the mirror, the stranger followed her movements exactly.

This had to be a joke. A weird, cruel trick. Someone had knocked her out, stripped her, put a wig on her, and replaced her mirror with some kind of video screen. That or it was just a piece of glass, and someone else was standing behind it, mimicking her every move. She wanted to throw a chair at the mirror. Who could have done such a thing?

No one, that's who. It was a crazy idea. The furniture in the mirrored room was identical to hers. When she moved slightly, the perspective changed exactly as it should. There was something else, too. Sheila looked down at her chest.

"No way!" she shouted, suddenly raising her hands to cover the large bust that had sprung from nowhere. "All right, now I know I'm crazy."

With a slowness borne out of her rising fear, Sheila slowly took her hands away and examined her new body.

Her new body.

The words gripped her thoughts and refused to let go. Her new face, her new body. Moving on watery limbs, Sheila climbed off the bed and went to the mirror. The stranger in the mirror moved to join her. She stared at her new face.

Her eyebrows were thick and rich, her eyes a startling shade of emerald, her eyelashes black and perfectly shaped. Sheila's cheekbones were high, her nose perfectly formed—thin, then flaring at exactly the right place. Her lips were sensuous and full, but not like Julia Roberts', better, more reserved than that. She had the bone structure of a high fashion model, along with soft, luminous skin, and a figure so magnificent even Mrs. Lang would be jealous.

Without warning, incredible rings of color flashed across the surface of her flesh, pulsing like the rapid beat of a runner's heart. The patterns scaled across her skin, flashing midnight blue, emerald green, bloody crimson, and sparkling gold.

The mask.

She had been trying on the mask!

Sheila's hands flew to the sides of her face, where the edges of the mask should have been. She expected them to claw into her skin and tear off bloody chunks of her flesh, but, instead, there was a blinding flash of colors like from a kaleidoscope and suddenly she was restored, the mask resting in her hands.

She dropped the mask to the floor and darted back from it. Looking in the mirror, Sheila noticed that she had been taller a few seconds ago. So she must have torn her clothes off because they hadn't fit any more.

Jesus, she had "hulked out," as Gwen would

have put it.

Sheila had never believed that things like this could happen in real life, but the evidence was before her. There she was in the mirror, her boyish figure and face restored.

"This is cool," she whispered, suddenly realizing that she already missed her new body and her new face. It had been the mask. Somehow, it had transformed her. No one would recognize her like that. She could have everything she ever dreamed of having, and when she tired of it, she could just take the mask off.

Sure, she thought. She would get tired of being worshipped for her beauty, of having the acceptance she had always dreamed of attaining placed firmly in her hands, of having doors of every kind opened for her. She would even get tired of having Ian take her in his arms and tell her that he loved her. *As if.*

Was that possible? Was any of that possible?

Sheila looked down at the mask she had dropped. It was possible that she had hallucinated the entire incident. There was only one way to know for sure. She would have to put the mask on again, go somewhere, and see how people reacted. Her gaze drifted to the clock. Ten minutes after seven. The masquerade at the Night Owl Club would be starting at seven-thirty. If she left by seven-thirty, she could make it through the woods and get there by eight. She would have to go on foot. Her mother would want to know why she needed the car, and she didn't feel like discussing it with Colleen.

Colleen?

The woman was her mother, she had never thought of her as Colleen before, only "Mom." Weird.

She would sneak out like she had when she was a kid, that's all. Open the window, climb down the vines and jump down to freedom and adventure.

Fine. But what was she going to wear? She was going to a costume party, so she'd need some kind of get-up.

On the floor, the mask flared into an array of brilliant colors. Sheila understood. All she had to do was come up with clothing. The mask would dress up her flesh in its beautiful, shifting patterns. They would mesmerize everyone at the party, especially Ian.

Sheila wasn't entirely certain how she knew this. It wasn't as if she had heard a voice in her head, or anything. She simply found herself, without warning, possessed of understanding. With total clarity, she knew exactly what the mask could do for her.

Throwing a robe on, Sheila cautiously left her room. She peered over the stairs and saw her mother curled up in front of the television. Her father's state-of-the-art headphones rested on her head. Sheila could scream for the woman and she wouldn't be heard.

Her heart skipped a beat, and Sheila stole into her parents' bedroom, easing the door shut behind her. Colleen was even taller than the new Sheila, and bigger busted, too. There was nothing exciting in her mother's drawers or her closet. Sheila wasn't sure exactly what she was looking for, but she was certain that she'd know it when she saw it. Glancing at the clock, she began to get nervous about the time. There was nothing here. She would have to go to the mall and buy something. For now, she took a pair of jeans, sneakers, a bulky sweatshirt, and a long black leather raincoat.

Back in her room, naked once again, the mask in her hands, Sheila wondered how she was going to pay for anything at the mall. She had a little bit of money in the bank, but no ATM card to get it out.

She would worry about that later. She had more urgent matters. Taking a deep breath, Sheila put the mask on once again. This time she did not lose consciousness. She stood before the mirror and watched as her flesh rippled and changed. The brilliant array of colors burst from her skin, a ghost light that kneaded and tucked, stretched and molded, and finally changed her into the ravishing beauty she had been a few moments before.

Sheila had no choice but to believe this time. She touched her face with her hands and started as the beautiful patterns of color flared once again. Her heart thundered, but that same calming wave of understanding washed over her. The patterns were hers to control. She willed them away. On command, they vanished. Giggling, she made them come back and disappear again, working the strange magic as if she were a tiny child discovering how to work a light switch. Delight coursed through her.

She slipped her mother's clothes on. Her face and body were beautiful, but she couldn't go to the masquerade looking like this. What was she going to do?

The mask tingled against her flesh. She could feel its gossamer touch even when the patterns of light were not manifesting. Suddenly her field of vision was consumed by a flash of blinding light. When her sight cleared once again, she saw that she was wearing something that might have come from one of her mother's lingerie catalogues. For a moment, she felt embarrassed at showing so much skin, but then she was grateful to have the figure to wear such an outfit.

The sweatshirt had become a shiny black satin push-up number with a plunging V in the center. Half of her cleavage was thrust upward and exposed. The bodysuit had no shoulders and she could feel that her back was completely open. The outfit clung so tightly around her hips and waist that she had to get used to breathing with it on. A touch of lace continued the V to her belly button.

"No way is this happening," she whispered, but she was smiling radiantly as the words left her fabulous lips.

The jeans had become a black skirt, slit down the side. When she moved her legs the right way, the fabric fell away and revealed them. Gold earrings and a matching bracelet adorned her, along with the tiara from the mask, into which her hair had been styled. The sneakers were elegant low heeled shoes. She couldn't walk in anything higher.

A ragged breath escaped her as she snatched up the raincoat and looked to her open window.

A moment later, she was gone.

Six

Ian Montgomery was bored senseless. The masquerade, which he had helped to organize, was a complete success. At least one hundred kids crowded into the Night Owl Club, all in costume, all, apparently, having a great time. The club's owner, Jake Demos, and his daughter, Jenny, had decorated the club with a vigor that made Ian wonder if Halloween was their favorite holiday.

Cobwebs hung everywhere, spiderwebs had been spun in each corner, and eerie red and blue lighting had been set up throughout the club. Kids could dunk for edible black apples, or kiss a crone, actually Melissa Antonelli, for a dollar. There were door prizes for best costume and a raffle for a new car that would end the three day festivities on Halloween, this Friday. One of the rooms had been converted to house a wide screen video set up, so the kids could watch some of the best and worst horror films in history.

The elder Demos had been reluctant to house

the three day event at first, but Ian's father was a salesman and the talent seemed to have been passed through the genes. A two drink cover had been set up and Ian had negotiated a one dollar per head kickback to the school fund for some badly needed repairs.

He *should* have been happy. Instead, he found himself fighting off a growing lethargy.

The masquerade was a diversion, certainly, but not the diversion he needed. He couldn't just put on a mask and become someone else, though sometimes he wished that he could. It seemed that he had been born with a host of unwanted responsibilities. Everywhere he turned, someone was looking to him for guidance.

That was fine. That was wonderful. Except— who was *he* to have this great "honor" thrust upon him? He didn't know anything more than the next guy. All things considered, he probably knew quite a bit less.

When people looked at Ian, they saw what they wanted to see. A tall, rugged boy with movie star looks, an athlete's body, and a grin that practically screamed self-assurance. He had wavy black hair, a square jaw, perfectly sculpted cheek-bones, a strong nose, and compassionate lips. His elegant blue eyes radiated sincerity and warmth.

Tonight, Ian wore the uniform of the futuristic marine from the movie "Aliens" named "Hicks." He loved science fiction. At some point in the evening, his friend Michael Roca was scheduled to appear wearing a homemade "Aliens" costume he had spent months preparing. They had carefully rehearsed a scene that would end, absurdly enough, with the two of them starting a conga line as the Miami Sound Machine's "Rhythm is Gonna Get You" played. It would be a blast, provided, of course, he didn't trip on Michael's damn tail. But even that could be played for laughs, so he didn't worry about it.

Everything was going great. So why was he so unhappy?

Out of the corner of his eye he saw a blonde wearing a fairy princess costume. His heart almost leaped into his throat. Ian raced to the girl, put his hand on her shoulder, and turned her to face him.

"Carolyn, sweetheart—" he began, then stopped dead as a chorus of laughter erupted. Standing before him was Scotty Glickstein, a long haired, lightly bearded classmate.

"Ian," he said, adjusting one of his healthily stuffed boobs, "I never knew you felt this way about me."

Shoulders sinking, Ian tried to cover his embarrassment by playing along with the gag. "It's been ever since that day in gym when you were all sweaty and your tee-shirt clung to you."

"I've wanted you, too," Scotty said in a breathless, mock-romantic tone. He swept Ian into his arms and dipped him. "Kiss me, you fool."

"Not until you get some Scope or something, man," Ian said, waving his hand in front of Scotty's face and twisting his features up in disgust.

"At least dance with me, then," Scotty said. "Please, I beg you."

"How could I refuse a request from one so fair?" Ian wailed. They walked, hand in hand, to the dance floor. Neither was surprised when the crowd parted and the spotlight hit them. It was a night for silliness, after all.

Ian and Scotty danced cheek to cheek. When it was over, they made a great show of engaging in a lover's spat. Amused, Ian realized that this gag could stretch on throughout his senior year. He didn't even want to think about what Scotty would get him on Valentine's Day.

Ian drifted back into the crowd, passing two Elviras and three store-bought Batmans. When he had caught a glimpse of Scotty in the fairy princess costume, he had thought that it was Carolyn Sugarman, his ex-girlfriend. She had worn a similar costume at Halloween last year.

At the end of his junior year, not that many months ago, Carolyn, his childhood sweetheart, had ended their relationship. She told him that her family was moving to Los Angeles and she didn't believe a long distance relationship would work. Since then, all the prettiest girls at Cooper High had swarmed to him. Every one of them wanted to be seen with him, but none offered what Carolyn had given him. She had listened to him; she had taken an interest in what was important to him. She knew his dreams and did not think they were stupid. He had been able to trust her with anything. That was rare, he was beginning to find out.

He only dated because his parents and his friends expected it of him. Part of him hoped he would find someone to fill the void Carolyn had left, but he doubted it was possible. He would fall in love again, his mother had told him, but it would not be the same; it was never the same as the first time.

If that was true, then what was the point of any of it?

It was at exactly that moment that he saw *her*. She walked into the club the same way he instinctively knew she would walk into his life, with a sense of purpose that would not be denied. She was dark-haired and beautiful, wearing a costume that made every boy in the club turn and stare at her in wonder and desire. Ian was not immune to this. He took one look at her and knew that he would kill to put his hands around her tiny waist and draw her to him. Then they would begin a kiss that would never end.

Ian shuddered. He tried to force himself to relax, told himself that he wasn't thinking straight. Any girl that enticing was sure to have a boyfriend already. Rational thought went out the window the moment he saw her sparkling emerald eyes, and the amazing patterns of light that snaked across her flesh, changing with her every movement.

He had never wanted a girl the way he wanted this one, here, tonight. Even Carolyn had never been able to elicit within him such a powerful and immediate response. He found himself walking toward her, and when he saw another boy start to approach her, he felt his body tense. If he had to, he would push the other boy out of the way.

He had to meet this girl. He had to be the first one to talk with her. If that did not occur, he would die. He felt like a drug addict, unable to control his actions. It was almost as if an outside force was guiding him; he simply understood what he was going to do.

That wasn't right, though. He knew what he wanted.

This girl. Here and now.

Ian reached her before the boy wearing the gangster costume. He took her hand, ignored her startled cry, and led her to an empty booth, where he stopped with her and found, to his horror, that he had lost his ability to speak. She did not seem taken aback by his abrupt actions. If anything, she seemed confident and amused.

She was even more beautiful up close. Her costume, if you could call it that, was the most amazingly sensuous thing he had ever seen. He could not keep his eyes from stealing downward and brushing over the contours of her magnificent body. Swallowing hard in embarrassment, Ian forced himself to look away from the swell of her cleavage, into her beautiful face.

She was grinning, actually pleased at the caveman-like act he had just committed. That made no sense. Women usually became incensed at such a blatant display of lust, and rightfully so. Instead, she seemed thrilled.

Despite her smile, Ian chided himself and swore that he would act with a bit more gallantry and restraint. He tried to smile. Yes, he could do that much at least. But speech was still out of the question.

Her soft hand went to his chest, brushing the nametag placed there. " 'Hicks,' " she said melodically. "I love that movie, too. Great costume."

Ian tried to slow his wildly beating heart. He wondered if his nervousness was painfully obvious to her.

You're going to speak, he commanded within the confines of his own head, *you're going to say something. You've got to, for heaven's sake. Even if it's the most stupid thing you've ever said in your life, you've got to get a dialogue going or you're going to lose her!*

"So," Ian said slowly, his lips practically numb with fear, "who are you supposed to be?"

Inwardly, Ian groaned. What a stupid thing to say. He sounded like Sylvester Stallone, all muscle and no brain.

The girl smiled. The patterns of light racing

across her skin practically danced with joy. "A woman of mystery. And if you play your cards right, Ian, I just may let you solve that mystery."

Ian congratulated himself on not fainting dead away.

Seven

Sheila had no idea where the words had come from. This was the first time she had spoken. She suddenly realized that even her voice had changed. That was not all, of course. Beyond changes that were strictly physical, there had been an altering of her attitude. When she started the long walk to the Night Owl Club, Sheila had been obsessed with the idea of seeing Ian's face when he spotted her. She had entertained fantasies of walking up to him, grabbing him, and kissing him on the spot. But, as she reached the club, an inexplicable feeling of calmness and self-assurance had swept over her.

Let him come to me, she had thought. *Even if it takes all night. Even if it doesn't happen at all. He's going to make the first move. If he doesn't, he's going to miss out. There will be others.* The way she looked, they would be lining up just for a chance to speak with her.

Sheila had been delighted when Ian had accosted her. She hadn't even spotted him yet. A good-looking boy named Brian Kretch who was dressed as a gangster had made eye contact with her and had been on his way to talk to her when Ian had appeared from nowhere and spirited her away.

This was better than any of her fantasies. Now she was standing alone with Ian. Though they were bracketed by dozens of students in costume, Sheila saw only Ian. Nevertheless, she was aware of the stares she was receiving from the other boys. In some strange, unnatural way, she could feel their gazes upon her, and that feeling gave her intense pleasure. Nothing, however, matched the joy she felt knowing how much Ian wanted her. His desire was palatable. It hung between them, saying more than words could ever express.

Words were no problem for Sheila. A voice whispered in her head and she repeated everything it told her. Simple. Ever since she had put on the mask, everything was simple for her.

"Would you like to dance?" Ian asked.

Sheila nodded. She knew how to dance. Her mother had insisted that she take lessons.

Seventy-one thousand dollars in debt.

No, she didn't want to think about that. The money wasn't her problem, it was theirs. Still, she couldn't help but wonder how much of that mountain of debt had been incurred for her benefit.

She looked at Ian and smiled. That was another life, one she didn't have to deal with for a while. He led her to the dance floor. Without warning, a spotlight fell on them. Sheila felt a twinge of nerves.

I can do this, she told herself. *This isn't hard.*

The dance was a slow one, which made it easier. She liked having all eyes upon them. They moved elegantly, as if their bodies had been made for one another. When the spotlight eventually drifted from her and Ian and fell upon another couple, she felt a sharp pang of anger. The spotlight had shifted to Yvette Depree, a stuck up, blond-haired, blue-eyed cheerleader who didn't possess half Sheila's figure and Jimmy Shulman, a grinning, mindless jock. Yvette had passed Sheila in the halls dozens of times and had never even said "hello." Sheila had been beneath Yvette's notice.

Why had the boy controlling the spotlight gone over to Jimmy and Yvette? Because Yvette was dressed like a good girl and Sheila was giving everyone what they really wanted to see? That didn't make sense. Yvette wore a chaste Little Red Riding Hood outfit, and Jimmy was made up to look like a wolf. How cute.

In that moment, she hated Yvette Depree. If that damned spotlight had come screaming down and had caved in Yvette's skull, Sheila would have giggled with delight.

"What's wrong?" Ian murmured.

Sheila turned her attention back to Ian. The warmth she felt at being in the arms of the boy of her dreams swept away any negative thoughts. "Nothing."

The song ended and a faster paced number came on. Sheila worried about bouncing around in her revealing outfit, then decided, to hell with it. Give them a show. Maybe Yvette could learn a thing or two.

Sheila had watched the dance shows on MTV and other channels. She had a pretty good idea how to handle most of the moves the kids made on those programs. The grace and ease of motion she experienced as she danced now was something she had never felt before. Now it came easily. At one point she had to slow down, because Ian couldn't keep up with her. She looked over to see what Yvette and Jimmy were up to. They had left the floor. Sheila took a great deal of satisfaction in that knowledge.

Finally, when both Sheila and Ian were covered in sweat, Sheila took Ian's hand and led him to a vacant table. They sat down and ordered sodas.

"That was amazing," Ian said truthfully. "I've never felt that comfortable dancing before."

"You just needed the right partner," Sheila said, mouthing the words that were being fed to her. "You're a wonderful dancer, Ian. I'd dance with you any time."

He smiled. "You, too."

Suddenly, Ian looked enormously uncomfortable. Sheila realized that he had no idea who she was. Of course not. When she had first looked into the mirror and seen her new face and body, she had also regarded the ravishing girl as a stranger.

"I'm Sheila," she said, holding out her hand.

He took it and decided not to let go. "Ian Montgomery."

"I know."

He laughed. "I know you know. That's what I'm trying to figure out. How."

"I've seen you around. You make the newspapers a lot."

"Oh. Do you go to Cooper High? I've never seen you before."

This could get difficult, Sheila realized. Suddenly, she knew exactly what to say. "I live in the next county over. Wakefield. I go to school there."

Ian looked relieved. "For a while there I was thinking maybe you were in college."

Sheila's smile was radiant. Only a few hours ago she would have had difficulty making anyone believe she wasn't in junior high rather than a junior at Cooper High. Now she looked older than she really was. More adult. She loved it.

"I didn't get your last name," Ian said tentatively.

The voice was speaking in her head once more. "That's because I didn't give it to you. Kingsly. Sheila Kingsly."

She looked down. Ian was still holding her hand, absently running his thumb over her knuckles.

He laughed. "I don't know anything about you and I can't take my eyes off you. I can't keep my *hands* off you."

Thank God, she thought. "That happens sometimes."

"You mean I'm not your only boyfriend?"

Sheila wanted to leap with happiness. He had called himself her boyfriend. This entire night was a dream come true. "I didn't say that."

"I really like you," he said.

"Same here."

"Do you want to go somewhere?"

Sheila shook her head. She liked it here. The attention she was getting not only from Ian but also from the rest of the kids in the club had made her feel wonderful. Only the blond waitress had looked at her as if something were wrong. Probably just jealous of Sheila's looks. She would have to get used to that, it seemed.

From the corner of her eye she saw a bright flash. Glancing over, Sheila saw Jack walking among the couples, his camera dangling around his neck. He was wearing a magician's tuxedo. The black cane dangling loosely from his wrist was attached by a black string. On his head was a life-size pink Energizer bunny. The magician's top-hat sat above the stuffed animal.

What was *he* doing here? The school newspaper had already sent a photographer. And where did he get the money for the costume? He and his mother were on food stamps.

She watched as Jack drifted over to the "Kiss a Crone" stand. Along the way, he snapped several photographs. He even took one of Sheila and Ian.

He approached Melissa Antonelli, his hands nervously stroking one another, and pulled a dollar bill from his pocket. Melissa, an attractive young woman with copious black hair, took one look at him and shook her head.

Jack's shoulder's sank. Fury rose in Sheila. That witch was going to humiliate him in front of everyone!

Her friend turned and was about to walk away when Melissa called after him. Jack turned and was surprised as the dark-haired girl in the sexy witch's outfit emerged from behind her booth and stopped him. Melissa took the dollar bill from Jack's hand and stuffed it back in his pocket. Then she placed her hands on either side of his face and gave him the kiss of a lifetime.

Eight

Sheila couldn't believe what she was seeing. Was this just another part of the humiliation? It didn't seem to be. Was it possible that Melissa actually *liked* Jack? But she had a boyfriend. Didn't she? Or had Sheila just assumed, as everyone else had, that someone as pretty as Melissa must have someone?

The kiss finally ended. Jack stumbled back, pulled at his bowtie, nearly tripped, and melted into the crowd. Melissa watched him go with a warm smile on her face. Then she went back to the stand and shouted that she was open for business.

"What was that?" Sheila said aloud.

Ian seemed confused. "I'm sorry?"

"Nothing."

"You mean that over there, with Melissa and that kid?"

"Yeah," Sheila said quietly. "Did that look like a mercy kiss to you?"

Ian shrugged. "There's one way to find out."

Sheila gripped his hand as he started to rise.

"What's the matter? Melissa's a friend. I'll just ask her if you want."

"No, it's okay." Sheila looked around once more. Jack had vanished. She noticed Yvette and her boyfriend looking in her direction. Yvette said something and her boyfriend, who had been sipping a soda, nearly blew the drink all over their table. He covered his mouth, nodded, and looked away.

"I was wondering," Ian said, "those lines, those patterns on your face, they're really fantastic. How did you do that?"

"Another mystery," she heard herself say. Her thoughts were elsewhere. She wanted to know what Yvette had said about her.

Suddenly, the roar of the music and the swelling tide of voices vanished. For a moment, Sheila thought that she had gone deaf. But there was sound. The bubbling laughter of Yvette Depree and her boyfriend, Jimmy Shulman.

"I know," Jimmy said. "I never thought I'd see the day that Ian Montgomery had to pay for it."

"She might not actually be a professional," Yvette said nastily. "Maybe she's seen 'Pretty Woman' too many times and doesn't know that the hooker look went out."

"Either way, it's pretty sad."

"Oh well," Yvette said brightly. "I hope Ian brought cash. She doesn't look like she'll take plastic."

The wall of sound that had been parted suddenly fell upon Sheila once again, swallowing up Yvette's words. It didn't matter. Sheila had heard enough. The little witch.

She was going to *fix* that stuck up, button-nosed cheerleader. She didn't know how exactly, but she would.

Calm down, she warned herself, Ian's looking worried. It was to be expected, Sheila realized. Yvette was used to being the prettiest girl in any situation. Sheila had blown her out of the water. She was far prettier than Yvette. She was the prettiest girl at the masquerade. *Wasn't she?*

"Sheila?" Ian asked.

She looked at him sharply. "What?"

"I was just wondering what had happened. You seemed a million miles away."

Sheila's gaze slowly crept back to the table where Yvette and Jimmy had been sitting. It was unoccupied. She looked to the dance floor and didn't see them there, either.

Good. They had left the masquerade. Now there was nothing to interfere with the wondrous, fairy tale evening she was sharing with Ian. Relief spread through her.

"I'm sorry," she said, squeezing his hands. "It won't happen again. Tonight, I'm yours. All yours."

"Then I'm either really lucky or somewhere along the line I did something really good to deserve this."

"You didn't have to do anything, Ian," Sheila said, wondering as she had a million times what it would be like to kiss this guy. Perhaps tonight she would find out. "You just had to be yourself."

He smiled, and from that moment on, the evening was magic. They danced some more, then went outside to get away from the noise and the scrutiny of the other kids. The stars were amazing. They were actually twinkling. Sheila could see their reflection in Ian's eyes.

"It's funny," Ian said. "All these Ivy League scouts come to the games, and I know it wouldn't matter to them if I wasn't all that bright. As far as they're concerned, I know how to do one thing. I can get from one end of the playing field to the other. That's the only value they see in me."

"That's not all you want for yourself, is it?"

"No," he said. "But sometimes I get the feeling that what I want doesn't really matter."

"It matters to me."

From his warm smile, Sheila knew that she had said all the right things. It was a gift she had never possessed before. The mask was helping her.

Ian shrugged. "Well, my dad's like the greatest salesman in the world. I know I've learned a lot from him about how to deal with people. He'd be psyched if I went into business with him one day. He keeps talking about it. He's got it all planned out: I have this great professional football career, make a ton of money, and he helps me start up a business with it after I've retired from the game."

"That's what your *dad* wants for you. What do you want for yourself?"

He suddenly looked sheepish. "This is gonna sound stupid."

"Nothing you say is going to sound stupid to me, Ian. Believe me."

"I want to be a cook."

Sheila steeled herself. She was determined not to give the wrong reaction. Suddenly, she realized that she shouldn't have worried. The mask clamped down on her, freezing her slight smile, which might have ruined everything. The last thing she wanted was for Ian to bare his soul to her and her to laugh at him for it.

"What kind of cook?"

"I don't know. I read about international cuisine, the great gourmet chefs. I guess it's stupid. I just like to make food, I like to experiment. If you want, I could cook for you sometime."

This time, Sheila's smile was not held in check. "I'd love that. You know, I was thinking—"

Ian cut her off. "Go through with my dad's game plan, make the bucks, and open a restaurant of my own."

Sheila nodded.

"I don't know if I'd feel comfortable with all that responsibility. When you're a chef, you can be a gypsy. You can go anywhere, see anything you want. You're not tied down to anything."

"True," Sheila said, thinking of her parent's financial problems, "but money's a good thing, and sometimes it's better to be the one in control. If you had your own place, you wouldn't have to worry."

He shifted a little from side to side. "That's way in the future, if ever."

Sheila let it drop. She wanted to ask him about his fear of being tied down. Did that mean he wouldn't want to keep her in his life?

She took one look at his magnificent eyes and knew that wasn't the case.

"What about you? We've been talking about me this whole time, I don't know anything about you."

"Mysteries," she said, repeating the words that were filtering into her mind, "are like fine wines. You want to savor them a while before you get a real taste."

Damn, that sounded so corny, but it seemed to have the desired effect. Ian was looking right at her, and she knew the moment she had dreamed of was coming.

He took her face between his powerful hands. "I'm savoring every moment I have with you."

"Then maybe it's time for a taste."

Leaning inward, Ian parted his lips slightly and kissed her. An incredible electric shock raced through her entire body and she returned the kiss

67

with a passion that had been building since she had fallen in love with him so long ago.

The kiss was endless, or so it seemed. Suddenly, a voice pierced the darkness surrounding them.

"Hicks! Get your lily white butt in here!"

They turned and saw a creature out of a nightmare standing in the club's doorway.

"Mike," Ian said with a laugh.

Sheila looked down at Ian's costume and understood. His friend was made up as the acid-dripping creature in "Aliens," in a costume that was certain to win the night's door prize.

"I'll be right there!" Ian called.

"Hurry up, it's close to eleven!" the alien cried, then hurried into the club, its tail swinging.

Sheila couldn't restrain a giggle at the sight, though, she had to admit, the monster looked scary enough at first glance, especially out here in the moonlight. Ian's friend had done a fantastic job. She told him so.

"Yeah, Mike's a goof, but he's really good at this costuming stuff. He helped with mine, too. I think he knows just about all there is to know about—"

Sheila leaned in and kissed him again. The second kiss was even better, because Sheila knew it was the last one of the magical night. She had to get home. If her mom found her missing, the woman would go crazy. Afraid that Ian would start asking too many questions, she told him she had to go.

"You're not going to come in and see the show?" he asked, his disappointment evident.

"Tell me about it. Tomorrow."

"How are you getting home?"

"The same way I got here."

He nodded. "Tomorrow, then?"

"Tomorrow."

She kissed him once more, then watched as he turned and walked back to the club's entrance. He looked back at her once more. She waved and blew him a kiss. He disappeared inside the club.

Sheila turned and started the long walk home.

Nine

Nothing could spoil this amazing night, Sheila thought as she climbed up the vines to her bedroom window. Not even the unpleasant prospect of having to remove the mask and become Sheila Holland again. Her window was open, and once inside, she checked to see if anything had been disturbed. There was no evidence that her mother had come into her room. Maybe she *had* pulled this off.

Sheila went to the mirror and surveyed herself once more. She didn't want to take the mask off. If she could, she would leave it on and look like this forever. She even *felt* more energized, ready to run a marathon.

Suddenly she was overcome by a terrible headache. The skin of her face felt as if it were on fire. Her hands went to the mask and she clawed at it. A searing flash of light exploded before her eyes and she felt an incredible surge of relief. The mask was in her hands. Her body had transformed. When she saw what she had once again become, a flat-chested plain-featured girl who could have passed for a thirteen-year-old boy, her sense of relief vanished.

A knock came at her door. "Sheila?"

Her mother. Sheila looked down and saw that she was wearing her mother's sweatshirt and jeans. "One second, I was just getting undressed!"

Sheila tore off her mother's clothing, grabbed at her nightdress and yanked it over her head, then kicked her mom's stuff under the bed. She ran to her dresser, opened the top drawer, and put the mask inside. There was no reason to hide the mask from her mother, of course. The woman had seen it before. Nevertheless, she felt better knowing it was out of sight.

Sheila called for her mother to come in. The door opened and Colleen stood there for a moment. She looked old. Older than Sheila had ever seen her. She wore her cleaning outfit. Probably on her way to a job. That, or she just got back from one.

"You have a second?" Colleen asked. "We need to talk."

Sheila tried to control her urge to panic. Her mother must have come in before and found her gone. How was she going to explain any of this?

Colleen sat on the edge of the bed with her daughter. "Sweetie, you haven't come out of your room all night. I know it's not fun to see your parents fight like this. It hasn't been any fun for us, either."

"Then why don't you stop?" Sheila asked, realizing that the issues at hand were far too complex for such a simple solution.

"We have stopped," Colleen said haltingly. "Your father and I came to an understanding tonight." She swallowed hard. "There isn't any easy way to tell you this. Your father's decided to move out of the house."

Sheila was stunned. This entire night, this fabulous adventure she had lived, had been strictly about her. She hadn't stopped to consider what could be happening here, at home. "Are you getting a divorce?"

"We're not sure yet."

"Money's that important?" Sheila asked. "Money's that much of an issue?"

What little color had been left in Colleen's face drained away. Her shoulders tightened. "Money is a part of it, yes, but lately, it's as if your father and I are on opposite teams, if that makes any sense. We can't talk to each other about anything, any more, not without getting into a fight. We both decided that what we need is some time away from one another to get our heads on straight. Maybe once we've both cooled off, we can give things a second chance. Your father's going to stay with a friend for a while."

"How long is a while?"

"However long it takes."

Sheila felt as if she had been shot in the chest. She wanted desperately to put the mask back on, to go running back to Ian's arms, but she knew that wasn't possible.

"He's not coming back, is he?" Sheila asked.

"I don't know."

Her tone turned sharp and accusatory. "You don't want him to come back, do you?"

"No, not right now. I need some time, too, honey."

Sheila tried to stay calm. She had friends who had been through this. She had always felt certain that if it ever happened to her, she would take it with a bit more maturity. Easier said than done, she realized.

"You just don't want him here, that's all it is," Sheila said as she leaped to her feet. "He's done every damn thing he could to make you happy, but nothing's ever good enough for you, not with him and not with me."

Colleen's expression hardened. "Sheila, calm down."

"No, I'm not going to calm down. I'm not going to be treated like I'm some little kid. Maybe you haven't noticed, *Mom*, but I'm growing up. I've got to start thinking about my future."

"Sheila, stop this."

"I heard what you said tonight. About my college money. Thanks a lot, Mom."

"Hey, wait just a minute, I wasn't the one—"

"No, you never are. You never do anything.

It's never your fault. Nothing that happens is ever your fault!"

Colleen's hands closed into fists and relaxed several times. She looked away from her daughter and went to the door. "I'll talk to you in the morning, when you've had a chance to calm down."

"Don't do me any favors."

Colleen stood in the doorway, trembling, about to say something else. Instead, she left Sheila's room and slammed the door shut behind her.

Sheila collapsed on the bed in tears. After a few moments, she got up and took the mask from her drawer, then lay upon the bed with it pressed against her chest. She didn't want this to be her life. If there was a way, any way, to make all her problems vanish, to disappear forever into the fantasy world the mask provided her, she would take it. No price was too high.

She continued to weep. Unnoticed, the beautiful patterns on the face plate of the mask mixed together, growing darker, and darker still, until the mask itself looked like a face made entirely of shadows.

Yvette Depree was in the parking lot with Jimmy when he crossed the line. She warned him that she wasn't ready yet, but he became grabby, insistent enough to become frightening. She told him "no" a half dozen times, but it wasn't until she began screaming that he let her go.

"Let me tell you something," she hollered at him, "when a girl says 'no,' she *means* 'no.' Can you understand that?"

He understood it, all right. He understood it all the way to his car as he got inside, cranked the engine, and peeled out of the parking lot, leaving her without a way to get home. She could have called her father, she knew, but that would not have been cool. Going back inside the club and telling one of her friends what had happened wasn't a particularly thrilling concept for her, either. The last thing she wanted was to give her "friends" ammunition to use when her back was turned.

The only other solution was to walk home. It would take a while, but Cooper Hollow wasn't that big a town. She could make it back in forty-five minutes or so.

It wasn't until she was midway through the woods that she became aware of how this would look to a casual observer. She was dressed like Little Red Riding Hood, carrying a basket. She looked as if she was on her way to grandmother's house. Now all she needed was the big, bad wolf.

Behind her, something rustled. Yvette spun, her heart leaping into her throat. "Jimmy, I'm not in the mood for your garbage. Come out where I can see you."

More rustling. Nothing moved. Nothing but shadows.

Yvette rarely looked at the newspaper, but she had heard someone once talking about date rape. Girls being raped by their boyfriends.

I'm not going to run. I'm not.

"Jimmy?" she asked, trying desperately to suppress her terror.

"Sweets to the sweet," a low, throaty voice called out.

Yvette shuddered. She tried to tell herself that the voice had come from Jimmy, that he was playing games. But she knew the moment she heard that terrible voice that it did not belong to her boyfriend.

She turned and ran through the woods. She ran for what seemed like hours. Every time she was close to finding a way out of the woods, back to civilization, her unknown pursuer corralled her back into the endless collection of nightmarish trees. She ran until her limbs ached, until the breath wanted to explode from her lungs.

Without warning, a low-lying branch sprang out of nowhere and cracked against her skull. She crumpled to the ground, dazed. Awareness came to her as she tasted the salty tears streaming down her face and realized that they were intermingled with blood from the wound on her forehead.

"Sweets to the sweet! Sweets to the sweet! Give me something yummy to eat!"

Dizziness and nausea raced through Yvette as

she tried to stand once more and fell instead to her knees. She looked around. The voice was getting closer, but there was still no one in sight. Where was he hiding?

All she could see were shadows that moved and danced with maniacal glee. How was that possible? There was no wind. She was perfectly still. What was causing the shadows to move?

"You thought you were the fairest of all," the voice said with a horrible laugh. *"You thought you were the fairest at the ball. How sad."*

This time it was right in front of her, but she couldn't see it; she could see nothing but the shadows. Suddenly, with a disturbing slowness, the shadows between the two trees before her congealed into the shape of a man.

Yvette watched in twisted fascination. Fear paralyzed her.

Get up and run, get up and run, stupid, this isn't some bad horror movie, you can get out of this, get up and run!

She tried. Her limbs were watery, her center of balance thrown off. She stumbled this way and that. But no matter what direction she chose, the shadows rose up before her and coalesced into the form of her stalker.

Without warning, the shadowman solidified inches from her face, then reached out and grabbed her. Its touch was colder than anything she had ever imagined. She was frozen in place. Her breath caught in her chest and she trembled violently at its touch. The shadowman's hands gripped her upper arms. Its touch was so inhumanly cold that it burned through her clothes and soon touched her bare flesh, which shriveled and steamed.

The shadowman giggled maniacally as Yvette screamed. She could see its face now. The shadowman had gleaming silver razors for eyes, and a mouth filled with sparkling needles.

"Pretty, pretty, pretty," it murmured, bringing up its hands so that she could see that its fingers were a collection of surgeon's scalpels. She screamed and tried to get away, but it held her fast. Slowly, meticulously, the shadowman brought down the knives that were its fingers and unzipped her flesh.

Ten

"Hey, you!"

Sheila spun and found herself staring into the deliriously happy face of her friend, Jack Kidder. It was Thursday morning and Sheila had successfully managed to get out of the house without having a discussion with her mother. The woman had been in the shower when Sheila woke. Sheila had dressed as quickly as she could, put the mask back in her drawer where it would be safe, grabbed her books, and left while the water was still running. Her breakfast had consisted of a stale pack of mini-donuts from the school cafeteria and a can of Coke.

The hall clock read seven-fifty-one. Less than ten minutes to first period geometry. Jack had approached her as she had walked toward her classroom.

"Isn't this a great day?" Jack cried. "The sun's out, no one's beaten the crap out of me yet this morning—damn, I feel good!"

Sheila smiled wanly. She wished that she could share in his enthusiasm. Unfortunately, despite the wonders she had experienced the previous night with the mask on, the knowledge that her parents were separating weighed far too heavy on her to let her be as happy as Jack was.

Also, she had left the mask behind and that made her feel extremely uneasy. What else was she to do, bring it with her to school? It was safer at home. The only person there was Colleen.

No, not "Colleen." Her *mother*. Why did she keep doing that?

In any case, her mom wasn't about to do anything to the mask. Why should she?

Because you said nasty things to her last night and she might want to get back at you, that's why. She might go in there and take the mask for herself. She's old, she's desperate, she'd kill for a second chance at youth and beauty.

No, none of that was true, her imagination was running wild. She had to get in control of herself. Her thoughts drifted back to last night and she said, "I heard you made a little visit to a certain masquerade last night, Jack."

He stopped dead. "How did you know that?"

Sheila shrugged. "I heard some of the kids talking about it. You made quite an impression."

Jack laughed sheepishly. "Yeah, I was gonna tell ya."

"So tell me," Sheila coaxed.

"It was great. It was amazing." Jack recounted the whole story, telling how he had spent the whole afternoon with Melissa, how easy it had been to talk to her, and how she had treated him as if they had been friends all their lives. He had arrived home late, took out what little savings he had stashed at home, and went to the costume shop.

Then he went to the club. The kiss, from his perspective, had been as mindblowing as it had looked. Once Jack started talking about it, getting him to be quiet again was impossible.

Sheila wished that she could be happy for him. After all, she certainly understood the emotions racing through him. Last night, her dreams had also become a reality. Ian Montgomery had fallen in love with her.

Well, sort of.

But that was different. What Ian felt for her was genuine. Melissa's feelings for Jack were, in Sheila's opinion, highly suspect. She had experienced firsthand the cruelty of these girls and had seen them play their little games many times before. Melissa could very well be setting Jack up for a nasty fall.

A voice deep inside her told Sheila that she shouldn't be worrying about it. She had enough problems of her own. Forget about Jack and Melissa.

No, she wouldn't do that. Jack was her friend. That *made* it her problem. He was in too deep and couldn't see things clearly for himself. He needed someone to watch over him. Sheila was determined to do that.

Jack's expression changed suddenly.

"What's the matter?" Sheila asked, disturbed by the unexpected change in her friend's demeanor.

He looked incredibly anxious, as if he had to deliver bad news and wasn't exactly sure how to do it. Then it came to her. Sheila put her hand on Jack's shoulder. "I also heard about the girl Ian was with last night."

"You did."

"Yes, I did," she said brightly. "Look, if he's found someone who can make him happy, that's fine."

"You're all right with that?"

"Of course I am." Sheila wanted to break into hysterical laughter. Naturally she was fine with the news. She *was* the other girl. But Jack couldn't know that. She was suddenly reminded of the photo Jack had taken of her with Ian. "I'll tell you, though. I wouldn't mind seeing what this girl looks like. I heard you got a real good one of her."

Jack bit his lip. "I don't know if it's going to come out or not. The lighting—"

"I'm not asking because I'm jealous. It's just—it would probably help me to end things with Ian in my head if I could just see the two of them together. Does that make sense?"

"Sure," he said. "Sure, no problem."

Sheila smiled. She had been trying not to think too deeply about what had passed between her and Ian last night. It hadn't exactly been real. The Sheila he had fallen in love with didn't really exist. She was a made-up body with a smart mouth that had come from God only knew where. But their encounter had actually happened, and that meant it wasn't exactly unreal, either.

"Oh, Sheila, I almost forgot. What time should I pick you up tonight?"

Wakefield. The Freedom International booth at the mall. She had almost forgotten. Jack and Gwen would need her help setting up the displays and she wasn't going to be there, she knew that right now. She also knew that she had a responsibility to tell him. Maybe they could get someone else to take her place.

Right. Like who? *Melissa?*

"I think the best thing is that I meet you there," Sheila said. "My mom said I could take her car. We've got a whole bunch of things to do and I might be running a little late."

"All right. That's fine." Jack glanced at the clock on the wall. "I gotta get out of here."

"Okay, see ya."

Jack was out of view when Sheila turned and saw her reflection in the main hall's glass trophy booth.

You are such a wimp, she chided herself. *How are you going to face that boy tomorrow?*

She almost laughed as the words "tomorrow is another day" came to her from "Gone With the Wind." She had watched that film with Gwen and Jack. Together, they always had a great time.

If she wasn't Sheila Holland any more, if she became Sheila Kingsly, they wouldn't be her friends any longer. They wouldn't know her. Her parents wouldn't, either.

Sheila had sat through lots of dopey movies in which a character had switched bodies then went back and tried to convince his former friends and family members of his real identity. Usually, he did this by recalling private incidents he had shared with the people he was trying to convince. She could see how that could work in a movie. There was a script. People had to follow it, whether it made sense or not. But this was real life.

If she were to abandon her existence as Sheila Holland, there would be no turning back. Of course, this was just idle speculation. There was no saying she could put the mask on and become Sheila Kingsly forever. On the other hand, there was no reason to believe that notion to be impossible, either.

Her reverie was broken as someone brushed past her. A boy.

"Sorry," he said.

It took Sheila a moment to realize that it had been Ian. She wanted to call after him. Instead, she waited for him to turn and recognize her. He didn't. Anger raced through her. She wanted to grab him and throw him against the wall for not taking her into his arms and giving her the kind of kiss they had shared last night.

Logically, she knew why that had not happened. He had no idea that Sheila Holland and Sheila Kingsly were the same person. But that fact did not quell her anger. It was true she looked nothing like Sheila Kingsly, but appearances shouldn't count for everything. There must have been something inside Sheila to which he had been drawn.

Ian was about a hundred feet away, about to step

into a classroom, when he turned and gave Sheila the strangest look she had ever seen. He stared at her as if he was seeing something impossible. Then he shook his head, shuddered, and darted into the classroom.

Sheila hugged her books close to her chest. She had no idea what had just passed between her and Ian Montgomery, no concept of what he had thought he saw when he looked at her. Nevertheless, his strange expression had filled her with a sense of hope that had not been there before. Whatever anger she had felt toward Ian had vanished completely.

As she continued on to her own class, an explanation came to her. For a brief moment, Ian had recognized her. Impossible as it was, he had seen beyond what the mask had made her and of what nature had deprived her.

Sheila's heart was light as she went off down the hall, unaware that in the spot she had just vacated sat a very strange shape. So long as it was unmoving, it appeared to be nothing but a shadow.

For a moment, however, it *had* been moving. It had taken the form of a man, revealing itself, just for an instant, to Ian Montgomery. Now it was fading back into the shadows, the razors that were its eyes dissolving into its blackness. The needles that were its teeth arced upward into a macabre smile.

The shadowman couldn't have been happier. Everything was going exactly according to plan.

Eleven

Sheila raced home directly after school. It wasn't until she opened the front door and threw her books on the living room couch that she remembered the photography club meeting. She felt bad for a moment. Never before had she blown off one of their meetings.

Well, it wasn't intentional, she simply had other things on her mind. Sheila raced upstairs, only dimly aware that her mother's car was parked outside. She had managed to put all thoughts of her parents' marital crisis out of her head and concentrate on the only thing that mattered to her: the mask.

Around lunchtime, the uneasiness that she had felt upon leaving the mask unattended that morning had returned in full force. She found it impossible to concentrate on her teachers' lectures that afternoon. All she could think about was a scene that had played endlessly in her mind: her mother going into her room, finding the mask, and taking it for herself.

Insanity. The mask was *hers*. It would not betray her. The magic belonged to her and she to it; she was one with it. Nevertheless, she was very afraid.

Sheila darted into her room, slammed the door behind herself, and went to her dresser. Her hands trembled as she eased open the top drawer.

The mask was gone.

"No," she whispered, "no way, it can't be."

She dug into the pile of folded up blouses, sifting through them with shaking hands. The mask was not hiding between the layers of clothing. It had been taken.

"Mother!" she cried, racing from her room and yanking open door after door. *"Where is it?* What did you *do* with it?"

She heard a stair creak. Colleen appeared. She was dressed for her day job, watering plants at offices. "Honey? Is something the matter? I thought I heard you—"

Sheila ran to her, approaching with such ferocity that Colleen teetered on the steps and nearly stumbled back. She regained her grip on the handrail and stared at her daughter in disbelief. Her daughter rarely got this emotional. The girl stood at the top of the stairs, stopping her mother from coming all the way up. They were at eye level.

"What are you, deaf or something?" Sheila snarled. "Where is it? What have you done with it?"

"With what?" Colleen asked.

"The mask, what the hell else would I be talking about?" Sheila seethed with rage. "You took it, didn't you? You want everything that's mine, and I know why. You're just jealous because I still have a future. I'm not washed up like you are. I'm not a has-been that never was, like you are."

"Sheila?" Colleen asked.

"Well, it's not going to work for you. It's only for me, do you understand?"

"Sheila, slow down. Are you talking about that thing you got at the antique barn?"

"That thing," Sheila repeated contemptuously. Of course her mother was going to try and downplay the mask's importance. She didn't want Sheila to know that she understood its power, that she wanted it for her own.

"It's in your dresser, where you left it."

"No it isn't. I looked there. It's gone. You took it!"

"Sheila, you're not being rational."

That was the last thing she wanted to hear. "I want it back!"

"It's in your dresser. If you want me to show you, then get out of the way and I'll *show* you."

Sheila stepped aside. Her mother took Sheila back to the bedroom and stood before her dresser. She bent down and pulled open the second drawer from the top. The mask sat on a pile of clothing.

Relief flared within Sheila. She grabbed at the mask and held it to her breast as if it were a child. "It was in the *top* drawer. I had it in the top drawer."

"All right. So? No big deal. I put it back in the wrong drawer. So what?"

The hardness returned to Sheila's eyes. "Why did you move it at all? You shouldn't have touched it.

88

It doesn't belong to you. I mean, you don't have any respect for anything that isn't yours, do you? You walk in here and go through my stuff, and that's just fine, but I can just imagine how you'd react if I went into your room and took something of yours without asking you first."

"I'd be furious."

"Yeah. You would. But it's okay for you to do the same thing to me. You are such a hypocrite. No *wonder* Dad walked out on you."

"Don't talk to me like that." Colleen's fury was brimming over. She closed her eyes and tried to control herself. "I came in and got your dirty clothes just like I do every week. You're too damn busy to do it for yourself. I had to move that dirty old thing. You could try cleaning that, you know. It might help it a little if you just used some polish on it or something."

Sheila tried desperately to calm herself. Now her mother was trying to tell her that the mask wasn't beautiful. Colleen must have tried on the mask and it wouldn't work for her. So now she was spiteful and jealous.

"Look at it," Colleen said. "It's filthy. I didn't look at it that closely when you bought it, but I can tell you, I wouldn't want to show it to anyone until I had cleaned it up some."

Understanding broke through the veil of anger that had been shadowing Sheila's perceptions. Her mother saw the mask differently than she did. It did not seem enticing to her. Apparently, the mask was cloaking itself, making it look unappealing to everyone but Sheila, so that no one would be tempted to steal it. That made sense, unless Colleen was lying. Perhaps she was trying to lure Sheila into a false sense of security so that she could take the mask another time. Anything was possible. Sheila couldn't afford to take chances.

The odd look her mother was giving her forced Sheila to realize that she had drawn far too much attention to the mask. If her mother was not curious about it before, she certainly would be now. Sheila decided a little play-acting was called for.

"I'm sorry," she said, though, in truth, she wasn't the least bit sorry. She tossed the mask on the bed as if it was worthless. "I know this isn't a big thing. I guess I'm still just upset after last night."

Colleen's expression softened. "I know this is hard for you. If you want to talk—"

"Not right now. I think the less I have to just, y'know, deal with it right now, the better. I've gotta kind of adjust to this idea. Dad not living here any more. The two of you being separated. It's hard. When will I see him again?"

"Soon I'm sure, honey."

"I didn't mean that stuff I said."

Colleen nodded, then looked at her watch. "I'm gonna be late. Dinner's in the fridge. Why don't we do something when I get home? Watch a movie or something?"

"I'm going to be out," Sheila said. "Um, Jack, Gwen and I are doing this thing in Wakefield for Freedom."

"Need a lift?"

"No, Jack's picking me up." Sheila shifted uncomfortably. Once the lies had begun, they had flowed from her effortlessly. "I'm sorry."

"Don't worry about it," Colleen said with a wan smile.

Sheila realized that some of the things she said had hurt the woman. For some reason, that didn't really bother her much.

Colleen went downstairs. Sheila waited until she heard the front door shut, then grasped at the mask and clutched it to her as she tried to fight off a series of shudders that wracked her small frame. It was possible that Colleen knew nothing of the mask and had no interest in it, but Sheila couldn't take that chance. The idea of having the mask out of her possession again for any length of time terrified her. The mask had been the answer to all her problems. Even if Colleen wasn't after it, someone might be. They might have followed her home from the antique barn. They might be sitting in front of the house right now, watching and waiting for a chance to break in and steal it.

Sheila went to the window and peered through it. She saw her mom walking to her car. No one else was in sight. Relieved slightly, she sat back down on the bed.

What was she going to do?

Then it came to her. Downstairs, in the garage. Her dad had a lockbox he never used. It would be big enough for the mask. The key sat inside it. Sheila ran downstairs, went into the garage, and started rummaging around for the lockbox. The garage doors were shut, but she could hear the sound of a car pulling up into the driveway. The engine idled for a moment, then was turned off. Footsteps sounded. Someone was at the front door.

Whoever it was, they didn't bother to knock. Sheila was frozen in terror as someone wrestled with the front door for a moment, then let himself in. She tried to tell herself that Colleen had forgotten something. That was all. Nothing to be worried about. No one was coming for the mask. It was safe. She was safe.

Then she heard heavy footsteps. A man's footsteps.

Someone was here for the mask. Where could she hide it? What could she do with it?

The mask tingled in her hands. There was one thing she could always do with it. Sheila slipped the mask over her face, forgetting to disrobe first. In any case, there was no time.

A brilliant of array of colors exploded before her face. She felt incredible power surge through her, felt her skin mold and shape into the breathtaking form of Sheila Kingsly. Her clothing had also changed. Sheila looked down to see how she was dressed this time. Nothing risqué. If anything, she looked quite normal, in a soft pink blouse and blue jeans. But the swells of her incredible figure were not hidden by the clothing.

That was odd. If the mask had the power to transform any clothing, then why had she woken naked, her clothes shredded and in a heap the first time she had endured the transformation?

Maybe because the mask wanted me to see its handiwork. It wanted me to see the body it had given me.

Still, the image of her clothing ripped to pieces as if a surgeon's scalpel had torn through the fabric remained embedded in her thoughts.

From inside the house, Sheila heard movement.

She had to get out of there. There were only two ways to escape the garage. Go back inside the house and hope she wouldn't be caught, or open the garage door. The latter would make a hell of a lot of noise. She had no guarantee that it would open enough for her to get out before the mask's pursuer appeared.

The footsteps came closer now.

She ran to the garage door opener and slammed it with her fist. The door groaned and the wail of tortured metal sounded. Before the garage door had lifted even a foot off the ground, Sheila heard the door to the house swing open. A man stood there in silhouette. She gasped, her heart ready to explode.

Idiot, she thought. There are a million things in here you could use as a weapon. Grab something. Grab it quick!

But there was no time. The man had already stepped inside and was coming straight for her.

Twelve

Sheila relaxed as the man walked into the light. It was her father, Gary. Jesus, how stupid can she be? Maybe her mother was right. She wasn't thinking straight. Even so, what if it had turned out to be an intruder? She should have been more concerned with getting raped or killed. Instead, all she had thought about was guarding the mask.

"Who are you?" Gary asked suspiciously.

For a moment, Sheila was taken aback by the question. Then she remembered that she was wearing the mask. Her own father didn't recognize her. "I'm a friend of Sheila's. She went out for something. Said she'd be right back."

She could tell from her father's expression that he accepted this. He had taken very little interest in her lately and would have no idea who her friends were.

The garage door was now open all the way.

"So what were you doing in here?" Gary asked.

"I heard someone coming in the door and I got scared." *That* was true enough.

"Why don't we go into the house?" He turned and

94

she followed him. They went into the living room and he said, "I don't remember Sheila ever mentioning you. What did you say your name was?"

Panic gripped her. It might have sounded odd to say her name was also Sheila. A name flashed into her thoughts, then retreated quickly. "Sarah Jennings."

"Sarah."

"Yeah." Sheila suddenly felt woozy. She gripped the arm of the couch.

"Are you all right?"

"Fine," Sheila said. "Flu going around or something."

That was really weird. The mask apparently didn't like her saying the name Sarah Jennings. But it had given her the name. Maybe it had made a mistake. Whatever. Sheila had no time to think about that now.

Sheila smiled inwardly. This was going to be easy. All she had to do was wait until he was in another room, then take off the mask. After that, they could talk.

Her father sat on the loveseat across from her. He clearly wasn't going anywhere. "What time did Sheila leave?"

"Just left. You just missed her."

"Why didn't you go with her?"

"I felt a little dizzy. Said I was gonna lay down."

He nodded. From his expression, she could see that he was not yet sold on her story. The man was in advertising. He was going to be a very hard sell. For all he knew, she was a thief.

Gary checked his watch. "I've got some time. Why

don't we just wait here together for Sheila to come back?"

Sheila frowned. "It could be a while."

"I'll wait."

Damn, Sheila hissed inwardly. "Look, I didn't mean to disturb you. Just go on with whatever you were doing, I'll just lay down." He didn't move. She suddenly became aware that her father was staring at her strangely. "Is something bothering you?"

He seemed extremely uncomfortable. "You look a lot like the way my wife looked when we first met. She's changed since then. Sorry."

They sat together in silence. Sheila felt as if she had been struck. There had been a time when her mother had looked like this? *Now* look at her. Colleen was over forty, working two jobs, facing bankruptcy, a divorce, and almost no prospects of a better life.

Maybe what the mask had to offer wasn't really all that wonderful. What was it Mrs. Lang had told her? She was going to look back on these years and realize ultimately that what mattered is how she saw herself on the inside, not the outside. Be true to oneself.

No, the voice that had fed Sheila her lines the night before whispered in the confines of Sheila's thoughts. *Your mother squandered her gifts. She made stupid decisions. The same thing will not happen to you.*

But it could, Sheila realized. Her father had once been a lot like Ian. He had been handsome with an incredibly bright future ahead of him. All it would take for Ian to fail was a single injury. One misstep and his future would evaporate.

"Look, you're one of Sheila's friends, right? Maybe you can fill me in a little on what's been going on with her."

Why? she wanted to ask. Don't you know? Maybe this was just a test. Well, it would be easy enough to pass. Then he would leave her alone long enough for her to take off the mask, become his daughter once more, and talk to him about his moving out.

"What do you want to know?" she asked.

"Well, how's she getting along? I assume you know about my wife and I."

"That you moved out last night? Yeah, Sheila told me."

Gary nodded. That one impressed him. "Yeah. We're separated. At least for now. How's Sheila taking it?"

"Shouldn't you be asking *her* that?"

"Maybe. But she's not here. I'm asking you. Besides, she'd be more likely to tell a friend than to tell her father. I mean, kids don't want to tell their parents anything. I'm sure you know that."

Sheila wondered where he had gotten that attitude from. Whenever she wanted to talk to him he was either busy or disinterested. If anything, he was the one who had never wanted to listen. But he was listening now.

"She said she doesn't understand why you two couldn't just work things out. She said if you and your wife just tried talking for once instead of screaming at each other, this might not be happening."

"Yeah, well, it takes two people to carry on a conversation. Two people taking turns talking and listening. Sheila's mother doesn't want to hear anything except the sound of her own voice. She never has."

Sheila nodded. There were times when she agreed with her father on that. But not all the time.

Gary apparently did not want to go on with that line of questioning. He shifted in his chair, crossed one leg over the other, and draped his arms over the back of the couch. Sheila had seen this move before. It was entirely calculated, meant to lure a client into letting their guard down. Gary's advertising clients sometimes came for dinner.

"Does Sheila have a lot of friends like you?" he asked.

"Like me? No. I like to think I'm kind of unique."

"Well, what I meant was—"

"There's Jack, Gwen, and me. No one else."

"Jack," he said, mulling over the name. "A boyfriend?"

Sheila gaped at the man. This was *crazy*. Either her father knew practically nothing about her, or he was delivering the best acting job she had ever seen. Something occurred to her. She tried to recall one time that he had been around when either Jack or Gwen had come over. The attempt failed. He really didn't know.

"She doesn't have a boyfriend. She's interested in other things."

"Come on," Gary said. "There's no such thing as a teenaged girl who isn't interested in boys."

You've never met Gwen, she thought, then realized that he was judging her based on his experiences when he was a high school student.

"Things are a little different now," Sheila said,

"than when you were in school."

"It wasn't exactly the dark ages."

"No, but there are some kids who really care about this country, about education, about issues. Kids like Sheila who want to do more than sit around talking about going to the mall or shopping. There are people in foreign countries who are being denied simple human rights just because they committed the crime of speaking their views. Some kids want to help change the world, not just take advantage of it. They want to be involved in politics and decision making."

"You've never heard of a little thing called Woodstock, have you?" he muttered. "Or Kent State?"

Sheila stared at the man as if he were an alien. "You were at Woodstock?"

He nodded. "Colleen and I went there together. But I want to talk more about Sheila. Her mom said her grades haven't been that great, lately. Do you think she needs tutoring? I mean, it's not a question of money, I just don't know how she'd react to the idea."

Not a question of money, she thought bitterly. *We're seventy-one thousand dollars in debt.*

"I don't think that's what she needs," Sheila said. It felt weird to talk about herself this way. "Maybe she needs things to just calm down for a while. Some stability."

Gary ignored this. "I'm thinking about having a conference with her teachers."

No, dammit, she thought, have a conference with me. I'm your daughter. Talk to me about this, not everyone else.

As the conversation progressed, Sheila felt overcome with a growing numbness. She knew she should have been pleased that her father was taking some interest in her life, but he seemed to be acting from guilt. He wasn't doing this to make Sheila feel better. This wasn't about her, though she had been the subject of the conversation. As always, this had been about Gary Holland and no one else.

Her father clamped his hands on his knees, then rose to his feet. "Look, if you're feeling sick, why don't you just lie down and wait for Sheila to come back. I can get my stuff some other time."

Sheila was confused. "You're leaving? Don't you want to see your daughter?"

"I think I need some time to sort through all this. You told me a lot I didn't know. I don't think I'm ready for another confrontation right now."

Sheila stood up. She wanted to rip the mask off and transform before the man. But the dizziness came back. She sat down hard. "You're not going to just talk to her?"

"Another time," he said, already halfway to the door. He opened it and stepped outside. "Maybe another time."

Sheila looked away from the door as it closed behind her father, leaving her alone with no one and nothing to comfort her. Nothing except the mask. She put her face in her hands and began to cry.

Thirteen

Sheila arrived at the second night of the masquerade fashionably late. The mask had given her a different costume tonight, one of her choosing. The venomous remarks visited upon her by that witch, Yvette Depree, had weighed heavily upon her. She had been determined not to give in to the pressure Yvette was exerting. The girl was simply jealous of Sheila's looks and figure. Nevertheless, her outfit last night may have been a bit untraditional and so she chose a costume similar to that of the Arabian princess from the Disney movie, "Aladdin." It was revealing, but not in a slutty way. The dancing patterns of light continued to spread through her flesh.

Ian was waiting for her when she arrived. Sheila kissed him in greeting. She looked around for Yvette, but the girl was nowhere in sight. There weren't as many kids as the first night, but the club was still happening.

"We figured the second night was going to be off a little," Ian explained. "The first night, everyone was curious. The third night, all the prizes and giveaways are going on. Tonight the only draw we've got is the Berserkers playing live. I dunno, the group's just too tame now that Gregory Rose is gone. I heard his girlfriend wasted him then drowned herself."

"I heard that, too."

Over the next half-hour, Sheila listened to the "noise" from the band. They played adequate covers of hits from Guns 'n Roses, Queensryche, Pearl Jam, and Nirvana, but with little spark or originality. When the band took a break she danced with Ian to songs they picked from the jukebox. After their selections, they picked out an empty booth, ordered sodas, and tried to cool off. Each song had been a fast one. Sheila had to wait a few moments to catch her breath.

"So how's the gourmet chef thing going?" she asked.

"What? Are you making fun of me?"

"No. Just wondering."

"There's a real easy way for you to find out. We're having a cookout this weekend. Just a couple of friends, nothing fancy. I'm gonna make Cajun chicken, stir fry some vegetables, with pork Satay on the side. It's good stuff."

"Sounds like it," Sheila said, not really sure what "Satay" was.

"So, you want to come over?"

"Maybe. I'd like to. I'll have to see."

"See what?"

"What I'm doing. What comes up."

Ian nodded. "Last night I told you some stuff I've only told one other person. Are you feeling any deep need to tell me something about yourself other than your name? Or don't I even get a clue so I can start solving the mystery?"

The mystery, Sheila thought, and suddenly remembered what the mask had instructed her to say when they first met. "What is it you want to know?"

"Well," he coaxed, "what is there *to* know?"

"Other than how I feel about you?"

That stopped him dead. "How's that?"

Sheila eased back seductively. "If you have to ask—"

"I don't have to ask."

She nodded. "I was born in a log cabin and had to walk three miles through the snow to get to school every morning. That kind of thing?"

"Sure."

Sheila shrugged. "I was born in a log cabin."

"And had to walk three miles through the snow to get to school every morning."

"It was damn cold."

"I'll bet."

Ian laughed. "All right. Another time, then. We have time, don't we?"

"Like I said, if you have to ask—"

"I don't have to ask."

"Good. Besides, you might think I'm boring if you got to know the real me."

"I could never think you're boring, Sheila. I *want* to know the real you."

"What you see, what you get, all that garbage."

"There must be something more."

"Do you really *need* something more?"

"I don't know. It's funny, I feel so comfortable

with you, but I really don't know anything about you."

"I'm a mystery."

"Yes."

"How do I know that when you've solved the mystery, you won't just go on to the next mystery girl?"

He smiled at this. "If you have to ask—"

"I don't."

They leaned across the table and kissed. As they eased back into their seats, Ian's attention was snagged by a handsome, grinning boy dressed like a pirate, making a fool of himself on the dance floor.

"Do you know Michael?" Ian asked.

Sheila said that she didn't.

"He was the guy in the Alien costume last night."

"Oh. All right."

"Yeah," Ian said, "you should have seen Melissa last night. She kept getting creeped out by Michael's costume. Every time he came near her I thought she was gonna just scream her head off. So he just kept going after her. It was so funny. I dunno. *She* didn't think it was funny. She was really scared. But it was just Michael in a costume. He was just wearing a mask, after all."

Sheila nodded. She wondered where Melissa was tonight. In truth, she didn't want to think about her or what she might be doing to Jack.

"I told him about you and he said he's dying to talk to you. Is that okay?"

"Well, sure, I guess." Sheila didn't particularly like the idea of sharing Ian, but she also didn't want him to feel trapped.

"Great. I'll be right back."

Ian rose from the booth and darted through the small crowd of students separating him from his friend. Sheila looked away and thought about the conversation she had just had with Ian.

Why was she so reluctant to tell him anything about herself? Was it because if she chose to remain Sheila Kingsly forever, her existence as Sheila Holland would no longer have any importance? Or was there another reason?

You're scared, that's all, a voice said to her, *scared of what he would think of you if he knew who you really were, what you really believed in. Right now, you're a clean slate. He can imagine you any way he likes. And you can make yourself over to fit whatever it is he wants you to be. Who knows, you could start talking about that Freedom International stuff and find out that he's totally turned off by it.*

Yeah, maybe he would be. *Isn't it important to know, one way or the other?*

A familiar voice interrupted her reverie. "Sheila?"

She looked up to see Ian standing near the booth with his friend, Michael Roca. He introduced them, and the guys sat down. Ian slid in beside Sheila this time, placing his arm around her shoulders. She loved being close to him.

Michael, a good-looking boy, sat across from them. Ian's friend had the rugged look of an action movie star. Sheila could easily picture him ripping off his shirt, strapping on a couple of Uzis, and racing headlong into an enemy camp, taking out the bad guys without so much as a scratch. He was tall, with wild black hair and dark eyes that sparkled with intelligence.

"So what happened to the alien costume?" Sheila asked. "That was really impressive."

"I almost passed out in that thing last night. I'm saving it for tomorrow. The big finish."

Sheila smiled. She had a hard time picturing this boy sitting in a workroom for hours, days, weeks, slaving to make the intricate piece of work he had created. But then she also never would have pegged Ian as wanting to be a gourmet chef.

For a moment, she could almost hear Mrs. Lang: *It just goes to show you. Appearances aren't everything.* A lancing pain pierced through her skull. She winced, then it was gone.

Michael stared at the gorgeous patterns of light the mask spun across Sheila's soft, luminous skin, a phantasmagoric weave of blue, green, gold, and red. "How did you find out about the Abassax?"

Sheila felt the mask grow hot at the mention of the word. She had no idea what he was talking about.

"The patterns you're wearing. It's Egyptian. You know that, right?"

"Of course," Sheila said in a small voice. She knew nothing of the kind, but she was very interested in hearing more. The mask, apparently, was not. It was becoming painful. Sheila felt the sting of a thousand needles boring into her flesh. She had to get it off.

"Ian? Ian, let me out."

"What?"

"I have to go to the ladies' room. I'm sorry."

Ian slid out of the booth and allowed Sheila to get away. She made it inside the restroom, thankful there was no line to get in as there had been last night. The bathroom was deserted. She studied her reflection in the mirror. The patterns of light flared brightly for a moment, bringing absolute agony to her face. Then, just as she was about to claw the mask off, the pain spread to her hands. She doubled over in agony. Sheila had read about arthritis, knew how horrible the symptoms could be, and also knew that it was not really an "old people's disease." It often struck teenagers.

A sudden, irrational thought came to her. This was Michael's fault. She had been just fine until he had appeared. If he were to just go away, the pain would leave her. He could go away forever, as far as she was concerned. She never wanted to see him again.

Without warning, the pain stopped. She took a moment to compose herself, then went back to the booth she shared with Ian and his friend.

Michael was gone.

"Where's Michael?" Sheila asked.

"You know Yvette Depree?"

Sheila sat down across from Ian. He took her hands. The pain was nothing more than a memory. "I know her."

"She came and got Michael. It was really something. She said she needed to see him outside for a second, like they were old friends or something, and he just went with her. It was funny, though."

"What was funny?"

"The way she just like—appeared. I can't think of a better word for it. Right over there, in the corner. One second I could have sworn there was nothing there but shadows, then I blinked, and she was standing there. Really weird. I guess it's just the lighting in here."

"Guess so."

"I'm sure he'll be back. All he talked about all day was meeting you. He wanted to talk to you about this make-up stuff. Whatever. I told you he wants to go to Hollywood and be a special effects make-up guy, right?"

Sheila barely heard him. "Uh, sure."

"Anyway, I'm sure he'll be back in just a minute."

She nodded, but she had an awful feeling that something had happened to Michael Roca.

Fourteen

Sheila came home feeling incredibly uneasy. She considered removing the mask before she arrived home, so that she could simply walk through the front door, but then she would be risking another confrontation with her mother which she was not up to. Besides, when she had removed the mask last night, the feel of Ian's touch had vanished along with her new body. Tonight, she wanted to carry the feeling with her for as long as she could.

Sheila climbed in through her bedroom window and gave a short, startled cry as a vine scraped her bare stomach. Hauling herself all the way in, Sheila looked down to see a thin red line across her abdomen. Her trembling fingers were about to touch the scratch when the beautiful patterns of light coalesced around her wound. The colors flared, became blinding, and Sheila squeezed her eyes shut. When she opened them again, the cut was gone.

Sheila stared at her stomach in wonder. The mask had healed her cut. She whispered, "That's *amazing*."

"That's nothing," a singsong voice called from the

corner of the room.

Sheila spun and saw a beautiful young woman leaning against the wall. She reached for the light switch and the woman surged forward, moving with inhuman speed.

"No!" the woman cried, her hand slapping down on the switch Sheila had thrown.

In the momentary burst of light, Sheila looked at the woman and saw razorblades bursting from jelly-like eyes, a mouthful of needles opening in a scream, knife-like fingers springing out like switchblades. Then the room fell into darkness once more and in the soft blue moonlight, the woman appeared normal.

"Don't turn on the light," the woman said softly. *"It hurts my eyes. They're sensitive."*

Heart thundering with fear, Sheila stared at the woman. She had obviously imagined the nightmarish figure. Her fear was getting the best of her. She was seeing monsters where none existed. The woman was in her twenties. She had soft, rich blond hair, gentle eyes, and a sexy, full mouth. Her lovely figure was clothed simply, in a white blouse tied at the waist, halter style, blue jeans, and running shoes.

There was nothing to fear from this woman. She was as human as Sheila. It came to her that just because the woman wasn't a snapping, biting monstrosity, she wasn't necessarily harmless either. She might have been following her. That was it, that made sense. The jealous witch! She knew Sheila's secret and she wanted the mask.

"Who are you?" Sheila asked. "How did you get in here?"

"*You know who I am. What I am.*"

"I have no idea."

"*You're afraid,*" the woman said. She came closer, her hand reaching for the side of Sheila's face. Her fingers suddenly looked long and thin, like surgeon's scalpels. Sheila stumbled back and fell upon the bed. "*Don't be afraid. I'm not here to hurt you. I'm here to help. I'm here to show you the way to getting what you want.*"

"Do I know you?" Sheila cried.

"*I am the mask,*" the woman said. "*I should say, I am of the mask. More than a servant or a slave, less than its master. One with it, just as you are on the way to becoming.*"

Sheila's heart felt as if it might explode. "That's not possible."

"*A mask that transforms its wearer is not possible?*"

There was nothing she could say to that. "What do you want?"

"*It's what you want that's important. What you want and what I need.*"

"All right," Sheila said. "What do you need?"

The woman sat next to Sheila. The room temperature seemed to drop and Sheila became frightened that the woman was going to reach over at any moment and take her hand.

"*I need for the mask to be worn.*"

"It is being worn."

"*You don't understand. You're wearing the mask, yes, but you're also holding on to the past. There's no longer any reason to do that.*"

"If I never took it off, I couldn't be Sheila Holland

111

any more. I'd have to be Sheila Kingsly."

"I don't want to sound cruel, but is that such a great sacrifice? Is yours a life that is truly so wonderful? Wouldn't you like to escape the horrors of your existence? You would, I know. More than anything else, you want to become someone else. The magic within me takes many forms, just as you can if you give yourself to it."

"I don't understand."

The woman gestured at Sheila's perfect body. *"If this form begins to bore you, I can give you another. I can make you over into* anything *you wish to become. Look at yourself in the mirror. Witness just a glimmer of the power you may possess."*

Sheila watched as her face transformed in the mirror. Breathless with excitement, she saw herself become younger, then older. She changed races, even sexes. Each time, however, she was beautiful.

"Do you recognize this face?" the strange woman asked.

Sheila stared at the mirror in wonder. She now wore the face of a Hollywood legend, a mysterious actress who had come from nowhere and become a star overnight.

"Or this one?"

Her flesh rippled and changed, transforming her into the image of a well-known businesswoman and entrepreneur who had created a line of cosmetics that had made billions. The changes came more quickly: a Pulitzer prize-winning author, a beautiful, respected newscaster, a noted humanist.

Sheila could think of only one thing each of these women had in common beyond their obvious successes — all of them were dead.

"Stop," Sheila hissed, suddenly frightened.

The face in the mirror returned to its original beauty.

"As I said, you should not be frightened. You stand at a very important juncture. I wanted to show you the faces of a few who came before you. Each of them wore the mask. Each went from obscurity and poverty to public recognition and wealth. You could be like them. You could be anything you want to be. But you have only one more night, then you must decide."

"Only one more night," Sheila repeated dully. "And if I say no?"

"I will take the mask and search again for one worthy of its gifts."

Sheila hadn't expected this. She thought that she would have more time to get used to the idea of becoming someone else. "What would I do for money? Where would I live, how would I get by?"

"You will never want for anything. Poverty will be for others. Hunger will never touch you. Neither will age nor pain."

"How could I go to school? Or college? There are no records —"

The woman held up her hand. Shadows stole over it, covering it like a shroud. The darkness vanished with a flick of her wrist. *"Black ink. White paper. Shadows and light. I'm very good with shadows. Anything you want can be yours. All you have to do is want it."*

"I want it. But I'm afraid."

"Change is difficult. I understand. I have a sugges-

113

tion for you. You have only one day left to wear the mask before you must come to a decision. Do not squander the gift of that time. Today, by using the mask, you learned secrets. Your father revealed things he would never have said to your face. Seek out those you believe to be your friends, and those you think your enemies. Find out what they really think of Sheila Holland. Learn what really matters so that you can come to your decision wisely."

Sheila watched as the woman backed into a shadowladen corner. The darkness seemed to envelop her. *"I will return tomorrow at midnight. You must make your decision by then. Goodnight, Sheila."*

The woman faded into the darkness. Sheila immediately leapt to her feet and ran for the light switch. One quick motion and the room was brightly lit, all the shadows dispelled.

She was not surprised to find the room empty, except for herself.

The shadowman attempted to restrain a giggle. Sheila did not realize that without shadows, there was no such thing as form. Though the room appeared brightly lit, there were still enough shadows for it to hide within. It watched as she stared at herself in the mirror, admitting her newfound beauty, considering its words. Its compassionate words were emulated from the memories of its victims. No matter. The task it had set out to accomplish was nearly completed.

This girl did not understand that the shadowman could take on the appearance of its victims. She was unaware that the flesh she wore once belonged to another. She need not know such troubling information. Not now. Not when she still had a decision to make.

The nightmarish creature knew that it should have waited a few hours to manifest itself. Whenever it performed its most sacred duty, the sacrifice of beauty, the harvesting of innocent souls, it became very tired.

Sheila had seen its true form when she had thrown on the light switch, but she had been willing to deny the evidence before her eyes. The shadowman had been afraid to reveal itself to her after she had gone to sleep. True, after resting, its powers would have been fully restored and it could have guaranteed that she saw only what it wanted her to see, no matter how much light flooded the room. But she might have thought she was simply having a strange dream.

Sheila sat down before the mirror, studying herself. From the girl's expression, the shadowman could tell she was thinking of Ian. It opened the doorway it had to her mind, a path laid clear by the mask, and found that its suspicions were correct. Sheila was lost in a fantasy in which she and Ian were married and successful, each of them pursuing their dreams.

Good. Let her believe her fantasy was possible. Let her believe whatever it took. She wouldn't be the first to fall victim to her own neediness. Nor would she be the last.

The shadowman relaxed. It had done well tonight. The creature allowed its consciousness to drift. What little remained of its body dissolved into the small patches of darkness it was able to find.

Within seconds, it was gone.

Fifteen

Sheila Holland was terrified. She walked through the halls of Cooper High with her books clutched tightly in one arm, the bag containing the mask in the other. The fear had gripped her the moment she woke. She was terrified to have the mask out of her immediate possession. She had made such an issue over the mask with her mother that the woman was bound to go back into Sheila's room and look at it. Sheila couldn't risk that. Of course, by keeping it with her, she confronted the very real possibility that someone might try to steal it from her.

She didn't know what to do. The mask wasn't safe anywhere. No, that wasn't exactly true. There was one place it would be safe, where *no one* could take it from her — not even the woman who had appeared in Sheila's room last night and had melted into the shadows. All Sheila had to do was put the mask on. Put it on and leave it on.

Today was Friday. An important day. She had a difficult decision to make. At midnight, the mysterious woman who had visited her would be back for the mask, unless Sheila chose to abandon her life as Sheila Holland and embrace her new existence as Sheila Kingsly.

Only one day in which to choose. Somehow, it wasn't fair. *Whoever said life was fair, kiddo?* The voice of her father, on one of the rare occasions when he actually deigned to communicate with her. Well, that was one person who wouldn't miss her. He would probably be relieved if she disappeared. But she worried how her mother would take it.

It was ten minutes to eight. Sheila didn't know why she bothered coming to school this morning. She had the mask. With it, she had endless opportunities to go out and experience life, not waste her time in this prison. All around her, students wandered aimlessly. Some clustered in groups, others leaned against the walls, and a few divided into couples who blocked out the world in each other's arms. Watching a young couple locked in a seemingly endless kiss, Sheila had no trouble picturing herself and Ian in a similar embrace.

Her *self?* She had no idea what that meant any more. In the fantasy, she wore Sheila Kingsly's body, not her own. Why did it have to be that way? Who's to say if she gave Ian what he wanted, a glimpse into who she really was, he wouldn't love her no matter what she looked like?

Yeah, right. And monkeys might fly out my butt.

Sighing, Sheila turned without looking and collided with a tall boy wearing a football jacket. She held on to the mask and allowed her notebooks and texts to fall. Grunting in exasperation, Sheila dropped to her knees and started to gather up the mess of loose papers that had blossomed at her feet. Fortunately, the frenzy to get to class wouldn't begin for another five minutes.

She was surprised that the boy with whom she had collided was crouching down to help. Startled, she realized that it was Ian!

"Sorry," he muttered. "I guess I wasn't looking where I was going." He looked up at her with his sparkling grin and electrifying gaze. "I went through you as if this was practice or something. I didn't hurt you, did I?"

Sheila shook her head. The urge to wrap her arms around his neck and kiss him as she had the past two nights was practically overpowering. Say something, stupid!

"I'm okay," was all she could muster. With Ian's help, she had her papers and her books together quickly. He nodded and walked off. He didn't know her. There had been no hint of recognition in his eyes. She thought that after yesterday, the way he had looked at her in the hall, there was a chance for her without the mask. Now she understood that she had been nursing false hope. The only way he was going to want her was if she was wearing the mask.

"Well, if it isn't the invisible girl."

Sheila looked to her left and saw Gwen standing beside her. Relief flooded through her. She needed Gwen's help. If she didn't get the advice of someone she could trust, she was going to go insane. Maybe she could talk Gwen into cutting first period with her, so she could tell her everything about the mask.

Then it came to her. *Invisible girl?*

"The mall," Sheila whispered, understanding crashing down on her. "Last night at Wakefield, I was supposed to be there."

"Oh, so now you remember," Gwen said angrily.

Sheila stared into her friend's face and saw the rage Gwen had displayed countless times when ranting about the people she loathed. Never before had Sheila seen her friend's fury aimed squarely at her. Panic gripped her. She felt as if she were staring down the barrel of a loaded gun.

"Gwen, I can explain—"

"Don't bother. Everyone has priorities, I understand. Y'know, stupid me, I thought Freedom International was a priority for you."

"It is."

"Fine. I mean, let's forget that Jack and I were worried about you, that we kept calling your house and didn't even get the machine."

Sheila thought of what her father had said the previous afternoon. He had come to pick up some of his things. After his talk with Sheila in disguise, he had left without taking anything. This morning, she had rushed out of the house without stopping to really look around. For some reason, the place *had* felt wrong. Her dad must have come back last night and taken the answering machine and most of his electronics. That meant the stereo and the computer were probably gone. Piece by piece, her life was being taken from her. First her college fund, now belongings that she had come to think of as her own. She hated it.

"I was out," Sheila said frostily. She was suddenly in no mood for Gwen's superior attitude. She must have been crazy to even consider confiding in this girl.

"Yeah. Fine." Gwen's chest rose and fell violently. "Are you going to be at Wakefield tonight?"

"No," Sheila said. "Probably not."

"Probably not or you won't?"

"I won't."

"Fine. The whole thing's off anyway."

"What are you talking about? What happened?"

"It matters to you, all of a sudden?"

"Yes," Sheila said, though, really the awareness raiser for Freedom International was the last thing on her mind.

Gwen shook her head. "You know, I thought with Melissa there to pick up your slack, it wouldn't be so bad. But—"

"Melissa was there?" Sheila couldn't believe that one.

"Uh-huh. It's funny. For a *pod person,* she's really not that bad."

"Wait a minute. Hold on. You had someone take my place. What was the problem? And why did you ask me if I was going to be there tonight if the whole thing got called off?"

"I just wanted to see what you would say. I figured I already knew the answer, but I thought I'd give you the benefit of the doubt."

Sheila couldn't understand this. She was fighting with her oldest friend. "That's real big of you."

Gwen's lower lip was trembling. She looked as if she might cry at any moment. Sheila was stunned. She had never seen Gwen cry. Never.

"Are you okay?"

"Get out of my life, okay?" Gwen snarled. "I should have known better than to trust anyone for anything. The only person you can trust is yourself. That's it. Everyone else lets you down."

"Are you saying this is my fault? That just because I wasn't there—"

"Goodbye," Gwen hissed as she turned and stalked off.

Before Sheila could think of going after her friend, she saw Jack approaching. She rushed up to him and asked what had happened the night before. Jack explained that Gwen had gotten into an argument with the people who ran the mall.

"She shot her mouth off one time too many and now we're all paying for it," Jack complained.

"So why's she blaming me? *She's* the one who screwed up."

Jack shrugged his shoulders and shook his head. Suddenly, an explanation came to Sheila. Dozens of times in the past, Gwen had been ready to go off and Sheila had been there to calm her down. It must have been like that last night, only Sheila had not been there to control her friend and avert disaster. But it wasn't her responsibility to watch over Gwen and keep her from causing damage. Gwen had blown the deal all on her own. If she couldn't accept responsibility for her own actions, if all their friendship meant to Gwen was taking her own failings out on Sheila, then to hell with her.

Sheila chose to change the subject. "Gwen said something about Melissa being there last night."

Jack's worried expression dissolved into one of absolute rapture at the mention of Melissa's name.

"She is *so* great. Can I tell you something?"

"Sure," Sheila said with growing uneasiness.

"Melissa and I are having our first real date tonight."

"You asked her out on a *date?*"

"Uh-huh."

"And she said *'yes?'* "

"Don't that beat all?" he asked with a goofy, put-on Southern drawl.

"That —" Sheila stopped herself. She was going to say 'that doesn't make any sense, I wonder what she's up to.' "That's nice, Jack."

"Nice," he said, his scarecrow grin spreading across his face as he loosed a hyena-like giggle. "Nice!"

"Okay, it's the most amazing thing I've ever heard!" Sheila said nastily. Jack's expression did not change. He thought she was just playing at being annoyed by this. She wasn't. All she could think about was Jack getting hurt. *That shouldn't concern you,* a small voice said. *Simply choose to keep the mask.* If she did that, Jack would no longer be part of her life. Not unless she befriended him as Sheila Kingsly. Somehow, that didn't seem likely.

For a long time now, she had felt trapped. The mask offered her a way out of this horrible existence. *The mask allows you to choose your new life and your new friends.*

"I'm happy for you," Sheila said, touching Jack's hand and leaning in to kiss him on the cheek. Then she noticed the time. Two minutes to eight. "I gotta run."

"See ya."

As Sheila hurried off to class, she couldn't help

but feel a little angered that Jack had said nothing about her standing them up the night before. She didn't want him to explode at her the way Gwen had, but it would have been nice to know she was missed. That, too, was because of Melissa.

Every time she thought of that little tramp, she was filled with an inexplicable anger. Melissa was setting Jack up. Anyone could see that. A girl as beautiful as Melissa would never go near Jack unless it was part of an elaborate joke.

Or would she?

Her thoughts in a jumble, Sheila darted into her classroom just as the eight o'clock bell rang.

Sixteen

Later that morning, in Mrs. Lang's class, Sheila found herself daydreaming. In her fantasy, she was married to Ian Montgomery and they were attending the opening of their first restaurant; he as the head chef, she as the manager. The place was packed. The wait was three hours long and people were lining up anyway.

"Sheila?"

She looked up suddenly. Mrs. Lang was staring at her. "Uh-huh."

"I don't suppose you have any interest in what's going on up here?"

"Not really."

The class broke into laughter. Mrs. Lang smiled. "After class."

Frowning, Sheila nodded. The next twenty minutes passed with excruciating slowness, as had the entire morning. This must be what it's like for a prisoner who's about to be released, she thought. Photographs of men and women who had been tortured and incarcerated for speaking their minds leaped forward in her head. Suddenly, she felt a little guilty. Freedom International needed all the help it could get. The organization depended on the volunteer efforts of people like her. Maybe if she had been there last night, things would not have turned ugly at the Wakefield Mall. A lot of valuable contributions had been lost.

Sheila started as the bell rang. She looked up and saw Mrs. Lang watching her. There was no sense in trying to make an excuse and get out of the "your attitude, young lady, has gone right to blazes" speech. True, she found it hard to picture the young and beautiful Erika Lang delivering the words in quite that way, but the meaning would be the same.

Waiting until the classroom had emptied out, Sheila went up to Mrs. Lang. She wanted to get this over with quickly. "Look, I know I shouldn't have mouthed off in class. I'm—"

Mrs. Lang interrupted her. "I was thinking a lot about what you said on Wednesday. I want you to see something."

Sheila fidgeted as Mrs. Lang opened her desk drawer and drew out a high school yearbook. It wasn't from Cooper High. Sheila saw the date on the cover and became confused. The yearbook was more than a dozen years old. Mrs. Lang opened to a page and pointed at the photograph of an overweight light-haired teenager.

"That was me," Mrs. Lang said.

Sheila wanted to ask if this was some kind of joke. The girl in the picture looked nothing like Mrs. Lang. The name was the same, Erika Lang, but that was where the resemblance stopped. The girl pictured was nerdy, wore glasses, and had a skin problem. She was also a blonde.

Then Sheila focused on the eyes of the girl in the photo. It *was* her teacher. Impossibly, this was Erika Lang when she had been Sheila's age.

"What happened to you?" Sheila asked.

"I went to college. Dieted. Had a lot of stress. I changed. People change sometimes. And I wanted to change."

Sheila considered this. She looked closely at her teacher's face and could still see some tiny acne scars beneath Mrs. Lang's makeup. Funny, she had never noticed them before.

"I got contacts, my acne cleared up, I learned how to dress, how to do my makeup and hair, which I dyed. I trimmed down. It wasn't easy, but it wasn't really as hard as all that either."

"But you said appearances don't matter," Sheila said. Whatever point her teacher was trying to make, it was lost on Sheila.

"They *shouldn't* matter. And when it comes down to it, I wouldn't have this job except for what I have up here." She tapped the side of her head. "But I know what you're going through. I mean, the PC thing to say is that I didn't change the way I looked because I was worried about how other people saw me."

Sheila nodded. Mrs. Lang always said PC instead of *politically correct*.

"The truth is, I was upset, just like you are. And I really didn't like what I saw when I looked at myself in the mirror. I didn't just do this because of other people. I wanted it for myself."

Sheila frowned.

"I mean, there are things you can fix and things you can't. You can't suddenly grow six inches taller."

Sheila smiled. *She* could. With the mask, she could change herself in any way she chose.

"The thing is, Sheila, as you get older, your body is going to change. In the meantime, there are things you can do. The way you dress. The way you hold yourself. You're already very pretty. If you want to, you could bring it out a little more, that's all. I could try and help."

The second bell rang. Sheila looked at the clock uncomfortably.

"I'm not trying to give you any great universal truths here," Mrs. Lang said as she rose and put the yearbook away. "I just wanted to give you something to think about."

"Okay," Sheila said as she turned and walked to the door. "Sure, no problem."

"Don't you want a pass?"

Ignoring the woman, Sheila left the classroom. The halls were empty. She thought about going to her next class, then decided against it. Listening to Mrs. Lang go on and on had shaken her. She went into the girls' room, which was mercifully unoccupied, and stared at herself in the mirror.

No matter what she did, she was still going to look like a thirteen-year-old boy. Mrs. Lang had basically told her that she could empathize with Sheila's unhappiness. Big hairy deal. The kind of fixes the woman suggested cost money. Better clothes, make-up, keeping up with all the trends — she didn't have time for all that, nor did she have any interest in it.

The mask would handle all that for her.

She opened the bag and looked at the mask. Everything Sheila could ever want would be provided for her. All she had to do was put on the mask. It hardly seemed like a fair trade. What did the mask get out of this?

It needs *to be worn.*

The girl who had been in Sheila's room last night said that. Why question it? Everybody wore masks. For Jack it was his silliness, covering up the loss and the hurt he had suffered. For Gwen it was her militant fierceness, shielding her fear of betrayal and her neediness. Her father put on his mask of authority to cover up his many insecurities. Even Mrs. Lang, whom Sheila respected for all the innate gifts she possessed, rarely showed her true face. Her teacher was wearing her mask now. That's why she enjoyed the attention her looks got her, why she liked being stared at by teachers and students alike.

Sheila had more in common with Mrs. Lang than she wanted to admit. She loved the way boys stared at her when she was Sheila Kingsly. The gratification was nearly as intense as the pain she felt when, as Sheila Holland, she was completely ignored.

Everyone had a mask. For some, it was money and power. For others, beauty. Whatever. But her mask could give her everything. Beauty and confidence. It could help her gain wealth and become successful at anything she dreamed of.

That was fine, but who exactly would she be? What would happen to the part of Sheila Holland she liked? Was there a part of herself she liked?

The memory of her chance encounter with Ian this

morning returned. He had not recognized her. He had been charming and polite, just as he would be with anyone. A part of her had been angry. She had wanted to chase after him, shouting his secret dreams to anyone who cared to listen.

But she would never do that. She wasn't really angry at him. It wasn't his fault. She was the one who had done something wrong. She had been born plain. Ugly.

A sharp, electric tingle coursed through her arm. She looked down and saw that her hand had slipped into the bag, her fingers touching the mask.

There was no reason for things to stay this way. Not when the means of changing her situation were this close. All that had happened today was too much for her, Sheila decided. She wanted to escape her problems for a while. That certainly wasn't a crime.

She took the mask out of the bag and looked at it. If wearing a mask was all right for Mrs. Lang, it was all right for her. People did it all the time.

She didn't want to think about it any more and so she raised the mask to her face. There was a blinding flash and Sheila Holland ceased to exist.

The door opened. Sheila Kingsly gave a warm smile to the girl who entered the room as she departed.

Seventeen

Sheila was outside, nearly a block from the rear of the high school. She could see the building and its fenced-in athletic courts, but she had no intention of going back there. She had no idea what she would do with today. The possibilities were endless. Maybe she'd go to Wakefield. Get a taxi or something.

No, that wouldn't work. She didn't have any real money on her. Well, the buses were always running. That would be easy enough. Or she could hitchhike. *That* idea appealed to her immensely. Certainly, it was dangerous, but that was half the fun. Just let someone try to mess with her. She wasn't exactly sure how she would do it, but somehow or another she would manage to defend herself.

The thought of riding in a taxi resurfaced in her mind. What was it the girl in her room had said last night? The mask would provide?

Sheila dug her hands into the pockets of her tight blue jeans. The mask had transformed her clothes, putting her in a tie-dyed halter top, blue jeans, sunglasses, and leather boots. She knew that she should have been freezing, that her outfit was bound to draw attention, but she felt quite comfortable.

She drew out the five twenty-dollar bills that were wedged deep down in her pockets and tried to muster something that could pass for surprise. Her efforts failed.

Without warning, a scream pierced the air. Sheila spun in the direction of the noise and suddenly registered where she had stopped to daydream. She stood directly in front of the deserted Grey's Funeral Parlor. Phillip Grey had died two years ago, leaving no heirs to the family business, which had been thriving. Death was one of Cooper Hollow's biggest industries.

The scream came again. It wasn't the kind of giggly scream of amusement heard at school. Something was wrong, terribly wrong. Behind the building, someone was in trouble.

Sheila dropped her books and raced toward the source of the scream. She ran the length of the building and squeezed through the narrow opening that had once been a walkway and was now overrun by vines. Then she stepped into a nightmare. In the courtyard, a gang of five boys surrounded two girls. Not one of them appeared to be older than Sheila. The girls were attractive, preppy-looking, the boys a rowdy pack of jocks. Two of them wore the same jacket Ian had had on this morning. The Cooper High Devils. The teens pawed at the girls, shoving them back and forth, laughing, teasing. The only way in or out of the courtyard was the overrun walkway Sheila had just come through.

Without taking time to consider her actions,

Sheila launched herself into the middle of the circle. All of the participants, willing and otherwise, were startled by her appearance. Sheila realized that if there was ever going to be a time to help the girls run to safety, this was it.

Instead, she held perfectly still, smiling coarsely at the pack of boys. Their crazed expressions faded as they looked at her.

"What the hell's this supposed to be?" one of them asked. Sheila knew every member of the Cooper football team by heart. This boy, and his friend who was also wearing the jacket, were not on the team.

Then how did they get the jackets, she wondered. Did they steal them? Were they handed down from older brothers? And why were they wearing them?

"Three's as good a party as two," hissed a sallow-skinned youth wearing mirrored shades. He wore jeans and a ripped white T-shirt, the same clothes that each of them wore, except for the two wearing the jackets.

Understanding came to Sheila. Their clothes were identical to help confuse the memories of their victims. The jackets were there to help focus attention away from whoever they really were. The faces might be forgotten, but those jackets would remain burned into the memories of these two girls.

This was worse than she expected. At first, Sheila had allowed herself to believe that these boys were basically harmless, that they were playing around and, if they were caught, they would run. Not so. These boys did not belong here. They came like wolves looking for prey.

"Now where were we?" said one of the boys in the

132

football jackets as he produced an ugly-looking knife. Sheila got close to the other girls. The boys started to close the circle around them.

God, Sheila thought. I should have just gone for help. What the hell's wrong with me?

Then it came to her. *The mask.*

"I'm gonna do something," she whispered to the closest girl. She had barely noticed them. A blonde and a redhead. The blonde was beside her, shivering with fear. "When it happens, there's gonna be this flash of light. Don't look at it. Don't think about it. Just move. Run like hell, get away from these guys. Get help if I don't make it out after you two. Understand?"

"I—I—" the blonde stuttered.

"Do you get it?"

In a tiny, strangled voice, the girl responded, "Yes."

Sheila reached up for the mask. She hoped that the act of transformation would be startling enough to leave the boys momentarily stunned. That might buy the girls enough time to escape.

Before her fingers could touch the edges of the mask, the boys stopped. The kid with the knife gaped at her. She had no idea what was going on. For some reason, the boys were crowding beside their leader, allowing Sheila to stand in front of the blonde and the redhead.

They almost looked *afraid* of her. That was insane, of course, but that's what it looked like. Why?

In the boy's mirrored sunglasses she saw the answer: her own face, shifting, changing, running like wax in a furnace. One moment she had the features

133

of Sheila Kingsly, the next a bloated rotting corpse, then something nightmare black, with needles for teeth, razor blades for eyes and scalpels for fingers.

She shuddered and her reflection was normal once more. "Get out of here. Go now and maybe I won't come after you."

The boys backed up a few steps. Sheila could tell from their expressions that they were scared, but not yet scared enough. The mask was feeding her lines. She heard them echo viciously in her mind. "Tell me something. You like fear, right? You like when you see someone that's scared of you. Gives you a feeling of power, right?"

The lead youth stepped forward. He was still holding the knife. "I'm gonna cut you."

Sheila wasn't afraid. She knew that the mask would not let her come to harm. Even if she was wounded, it would heal her. Nevertheless, the prospect of being stabbed did not appeal to her.

An idea forced its way into her head. She smiled and gave in to the mask's wishes. "I bet you're scared of dying, aren't you? It's something you think only happens to other people. That's not true. Wanna see yourself dead? Look!"

Sheila could feel her flesh rippling. Her face was changing. The boy in the shades moved forward slightly, enough to give Sheila a look at herself in the reflection.

She now looked exactly like the boy in the lead, only her face—his face—looked as if it had been underwater for days. It was green, partially eaten, strips of flesh dangling from the bone.

"Gonna cut you!" the boy screamed, launching

134

himself at her. The youth with the mirrored sunglasses caught him and dragged him back.

"No way, man," Shades snarled. "No way. You cut her, she'll just bleed acid, she'll just laugh at you!"

"He's right," Sheila said, spitting on the ground. A small section of the concrete walk hissed and dissolved. A thin funnel of white smoke rose from the ground. How in the hell had she done that?

The boy dropped his knife and peed in his pants. All of the boys backed up as Sheila advanced toward them. "You're going to get out of here. You're never coming to Cooper Hollow again. Understand? If you do, I'll know about it, and I'll cut you. That goes for all of you! Do you understand? Does that make *sense* to you?"

The absolute terror in their eyes told Sheila that it did. *"Get out!"*

She could not restrain a smile as the boys ran from the courtyard.

Eighteen

Sheila returned to Cooper High with Lisa and Claire, the girls she had rescued. They had been behind Sheila and were unaware of the tricks she had used to make their assailants run off. All they knew was that somehow, miraculously, this girl had come from nowhere and saved them from a violent assault. Sheila also thought of herself as heroic until she talked the girls out of going to the police and reporting the incident. That had been wrong. Selfish. She didn't want to spend her day in a police station, filling out forms, being made to answer questions that she could not possibly answer. After all, she was Sheila Kingsly at the moment, and that meant she had no address, social security number, or life beyond what the mask gave her.

Those boys would find other victims.

Not necessarily, the voice of the mask whispered in her mind. *They know we can take on any guise. When they approach any woman they'll wonder if it's you in disguise.*

That might not be enough to dissuade them, she

knew, but it would have to be enough. She *had* gone to the aid of these girls when it didn't really serve her own interests. They were grateful. Why complicate things?

Somehow, she wasn't convinced.

The voice inside her head grew impatient. *Face it, Sheila. You weren't trying to be a hero, You were just trying to save yourself.*

Oh, really? Then why did I rush in there in the first place?

You know why. For the thrill.

"Sheila?"

She turned to look at Claire, the blonde. They were sitting in the school's theater, which doubled as a study hall. A few dozen students were scattered throughout. None were close to the trio of girls. "Sorry."

"I don't know how to say this, I'll just say it, okay? I am forever in your debt. God, that sounds so corny. Like, get real. I dunno how else to say it."

"You don't have to. It's all right."

"No, it isn't. Really," Lisa, the redhead added. "What you did was amazing. Facing those guys down. I mean, maybe they weren't really serious, or else they wouldn't have run away, but—"

Anger flickered briefly in Sheila's eyes. "Not serious? That *knife* wasn't serious?"

Lisa blanched. "What I mean is—I'm sorry. I don't know what I mean. Maybe I'm just trying to convince myself that it never really happened."

"It happened."

Both Claire and Lisa nodded.

"All that matters is that you're both okay," Sheila

said wearily.

"I'm fine," Claire said. "I'm curious, though. Who are you? I mean, I saw you at the masquerade with Ian the past two nights, and there're all these rumors going around, but no one has any idea who you are."

Sheila smiled. Suddenly, the words of the mysterious young woman from the previous night returned to her. She could use the mask to find out what people really thought of her. "Do you know a girl named Sheila Holland? I don't know much about her, I'm just supposed to meet her."

"Sure, everyone knows her," Lisa said.

Sheila tightened, preparing herself for the onslaught of insults. *She's a nerd, a brain, a stuck-up little jerk no one likes.*

"Yeah, Sheila's really cool," Lisa said. "It takes a lot of guts not to care what everybody thinks, y'know?"

"Uh," Sheila said, stunned.

"Yeah, I mean, you know what it's like," Claire added. "You have all this pressure on you all the time. I mean, if it's me, if I don't wear the right things, see the right people—you understand. I dunno, I really envy someone like that. She has all this freedom. She doesn't have to worry about all this stuff. Sometimes I wish I just had the guts to do what she does, just be myself, just take care of what I care about instead of always trying to please everybody."

Sheila could not believe what she was hearing. Incredulously, she said, "You *like* Sheila Holland?"

Claire and Lisa looked at each other as if they had just made a monumental error. Clearly, they did not want to anger the girl who had saved them.

"I mean, that's okay, I'm just —" Sheila winced as the terrible pain she had experienced last night returned to her. Needles seemed to be driven through her face. The pain subsided as quickly as it had risen. She had the odd feeling the mask did not want her to continue with this after all.

A male voice sounded. *"Sheila."*

She turned in her chair and saw Ian sitting in the row behind her. "I'd know your voice anywhere."

Claire and Lisa giggled and excused themselves. "See you at the party tonight!" one of them called.

Ian smiled. "Can I sit with you?"

"What do you think?"

He climbed over the seat and eased down next to her, taking her hand in his as he leaned over and kissed her. The mask certainly had no objection to this, it seemed.

"I didn't expect to see you until tonight," Ian said. "What are you doing here?"

"I came to see a friend."

"Oh yeah? Who's that?"

She decided to go for broke. "Sheila Holland. Do you know her?"

Ian nodded thoughtfully. "I know her name. I have this one friend who talks about her a lot, he's got this real crush on her."

Sheila couldn't believe what she was hearing.

"I don't know her, but I think if I did, I'd probably like her."

Sheila swallowed hard. "You mean, you don't know her to *see* her?"

"I guess that's pretty bad, huh? I mean, I get

people coming up to me all the time and—"

"No, I understand," she said excitedly. "But you think you would like her, if you got to know her?"

"I guess so. Why? Is she a friend of yours?"

"Yeah," Sheila said, suddenly picturing the masquerade tonight. Sheila Kingsly could stand Ian up and send Sheila Holland in her place. The pain flared within her flesh once again. Sheila ignored it. "You really think you'd like her?"

"Maybe. But I love *you*."

"You do," she whispered numbly. The sudden agony faded. Sheila looked into Ian's face. His confident expression wavered slightly. He was wondering if he had done the right thing by telling her how he felt. She had to do something, had to say something to let him know everything was all right.

The truth. That might work. "I've loved you from the first moment I saw you."

His face became bright once again and they came together in a fierce kiss. When their lips finally parted, Sheila leaned down and rested her head on his chest. She *had* fallen in love with him the first time she had seen him. She could remember the moment perfectly.

"It was here," she said. "There was this student, Jack Kidder, and he was getting picked on by Freddie Semblowski. Freddie and his friends grabbed this book Jack's father had sent him and they were throwing it all over the place. Jack was trying not to lose it completely, but his dad's been in jail a long time and there was this note written in the front of the book. It was the only thing his father had written to him since he went away.

"Freddie had the book and one of his friends was holding Jack by the ankles, shaking him, trying to make the change and everything come out of Jack's pockets. Big fun, y'know. Then, like, out of nowhere, you were there. You made them stop. You got Jack's book back for him, then you took Freddie and his idiot friends to the other side of the auditorium and you talked to them. I don't know what you said, but they never bothered Jack again.

"It was like something out of a fairy tale. I'll never forget it."

She raised her head and saw the confusion in Ian's eyes.

"I remember that," he said, "but where were you? You said you don't go to school here."

Sheila swallowed hard. She had been there, all right, but as Sheila Holland, not Sheila Kingsly. "I was visiting, like I am today. You know, sometimes they send files and stuff back and forth from the different schools and they give students time off to bring the stuff over. It was like that."

"Oh."

Sheila relaxed. Ian believed her. It was going to be all right. She looked away and saw three students sitting together several rows down. Gwen, Jack, and Melissa. They were laughing. All three of them. That should have been Sheila down there, not Melissa. What was happening to her life?

"I have to go now," Sheila said, unable to bear the sight of Jack and Gwen having fun with Melissa.

Ian sat bolt upright. "I thought maybe we could just talk for a while. I still don't know anything about you, really."

"Tonight. Tonight, at midnight. I'll tell you everything. Can you wait that long?"

"I'd wait forever, if I had to."

She kissed him and hurried out of the auditorium.

Nineteen

Sheila took the bus to Wakefield and hung around the mall the rest of the afternoon. She bought several outfits with the money she had found in her jeans and sat through a bargain matinee. By the time she arrived home, she couldn't even remember what movie she had gone to see. It was all a blur. Her mind had been racing all day.

She had expected those girls to hate Sheila Holland. Instead, they admired her. Ian said that he would probably care for Sheila Holland, but he *loved* Sheila Kingsly. What would he do if she took the mask off in front of him? Would he become angry at her? Feel betrayed and humiliated? Or would he simply look at her as if she were a Martian or something, the way the boys in the courtyard had?

Maybe her first idea had been the right one. Show up at the masquerade as Sheila Holland and tell Ian that Sheila Kingsly couldn't make it. Funny — when she had been a little girl, playing with her friends, she had played a similar game. She would pretend to be two people, first talking to her playmates in the

143

backyard as herself, then running around the length of the house and returning as someone completely different. The twin sister or the cousin. It had been a fun game.

This was not a game. This was her life. She had only a few hours left to decide if she would renounce her existence as Sheila Holland and embrace a new life as Sheila Kingsly. Here it was, five-thirty in the afternoon, and she was no closer to making the decision than she had been this morning. She considered taking the mask off, but it seemed like too much effort.

Sheila was upstairs, in her room, when she heard a soft knock. Before she could respond, the door opened and her mother came in. Weird. She was certain that she had been alone in the house.

Colleen looked tense. She had just come in from one of her cleaning jobs and she was evidently geared up for a fight.

Not now, Sheila thought. Just not now, please.

"Honey, we need to talk."

God, she dreaded those words. "Mom, can we do it tomorrow? I'm really not feeling too good."

Colleen leaned up against the wall. "We're going to talk right now. This has gone on long enough."

"Really, mom, tomorrow—"

"Now."

Sheila hung her shoulders in defeat. Something was nagging at her, something about this was wrong, terribly wrong, but, for the life of her, she couldn't tell what it was. "All right. Now."

"Things have to change around here, young lady. First off, there's the matter of your attitude."

"My attitude?"

"Yes. I'm tired of being treated as if I was nothing more than your servant. From this point on, you're going to show me some respect."

"Mom—"

Colleen's hand shot out and closed on Sheila's face, her fingers digging into the hollows of her daughter's cheeks. "Listen to me good, you ungrateful little witch. You are to address me as 'ma'am.' Do you understand that?"

Sheila's heart felt ready to explode. "Ma'am?" What, had her mother gone crazy? Colleen's grip tightened.

"Do you understand? Do you?"

"Yes!"

Colleen released her hold. "Good. Because I've had about enough of you, okay, kid? The way this world works is that you look out for yourself. You get what you can, screw everyone else. I'm tired of your whining. So we took your college fund. So what? You think you're going to amount to anything? You don't know what you want to be. Nothing holds your interest more than a week. If it weren't for you, Gary and I wouldn't even be in this goddamned situation."

"That's not true," Sheila said, trying to hold back the rush of tears struggling for release.

Colleen raised her hand as if she were about to strike Sheila.

"Ma'am!" Sheila cried. "It's not true, ma'am. Not true."

Colleen lowered her hand. "You sniveling, worthless little crybaby. Christ, I wish you had never

145

been born."

Shaking her head in disgust, Colleen stormed out of the room, slamming the door behind her. Sheila overcame her shock long enough to run to the door and rip it open.

The shadowladen hallway was empty. Colleen's door was closed. Sheila considered going into her mother's bedroom to confront the woman, then thought better of it. She went back inside her room, slammed her door, and locked it behind her.

Sheila did not see the cluster of shadows crouched at the other end of the hall, away from the main window. They rose briefly, coalescing into the form of a human. Images rippled through the shadowman. The face and form of the mysterious young woman from the previous night. Then the perfect image of Colleen Holland, who would not be home for hours.

The shadowman released the woman's image and assumed its own nightmarish form. Taking the shape of a human it had not killed was difficult for the creature. It had been on the brink of exhaustion when the mask had summoned it for this last exercise.

The powers of the mask and its servant were interrelated. When the shadowman fed, the mask was energized. Conversely, when it hungered, the mask was weakened. The shadowman was starved. Tonight, it would feast. Sheila would choose the final victim tonight, then the mask and the shadowman would be able to rest for a time. The selection of a new host had never been this difficult before.

It worried that it would not have the energy to do what it must tonight. Somehow it had to hold on. But that was impossible. It needed rest. Already it could feel itself dissolving into the shadows.

A cold, angry fist, closed over its dimming consciousness. It realized it had made a mistake. A potentially fatal flaw. It hoped the mask would be able to avert Sheila's attention from its horrible error. If not, their work here might well be undone.

The shadowman's last thought was that it prayed it would wake in time not to disappoint its master.

All that was left was darkness.

It was all too much for Sheila to take. Her father wouldn't speak to her. Her mother wished she had never been born. Gwen hated her and Ian had stared right into her eyes and had not recognized her.

Her only real friend was Jack. He was the only one who knew her and accepted her fully. She had to talk to Jack.

With trembling hands, Sheila picked up her phone and dialed Jack's number. The call was answered on the third ring. "Hello?"

It was Jack's mother. "Hi, Mrs. Kidder. Can I talk to Jack, please?"

There was a slight pause. "Who is this?"

Sheila felt a sudden burst of exasperation, but she tried to keep her tone from becoming nasty or impatient. "It's Sheila."

"Really? You don't sound like yourself."

Sheila looked to her mirror. She was still wearing

the mask. She hadn't taken it off since lunchtime. Clearing her throat, Sheila said, "I've got a cold. And we're having problems with the phone lines."

"Oh. Well, Jack's not here."

Sheila's heart sank. She needed him and he wasn't there, just like everyone else. Who was she going to call now? Gwen? Not likely. "Do you know when he'll be in?"

"I couldn't say. I let him borrow the car and he's already got his costume. If you're going to the Night Owl tonight, you'll probably find him there with Melissa."

The name thudded in Sheila's head. "Melissa."

"Isn't it wonderful, the way the two of them are getting along? That girl is the best thing that's ever happened to my son. I'm already thinking wedding thoughts. Isn't that crazy? I guess I'm just really happy that Jack's found someone who really appreciates him. I've never seen him like this before. He's so happy. It's so *wonderful*."

"Yeah," Sheila said. "It's just great." This she didn't need to hear. "I gotta go. Would you please tell him I called if he stops back?"

"I will."

"Thanks. Bye!" Sheila hung up the phone. She sat quietly for almost ten minutes before she exploded in rage. Melissa Antonelli. It always came back to her, didn't it? Gwen was known to despise girls like Melissa on sight, but she accepted the girl, even seemed anxious to have Melissa take Sheila's place within their group. Sheila couldn't even talk to Jack any more. Even when he was with her, his thoughts were on Melissa.

148

All of that would be fine, except that Melissa was playing Jack for a fool. She was going to hurt him so badly he might never recover.

Hadn't he looked in a mirror lately? There was no way a girl like Melissa Antonelli would honestly fall in love with Jack; that kind of thing just didn't happen. The pretty people stuck with their own kind. That's why she really didn't stand a chance with Ian as Sheila Holland. He wasn't stuck up or rotten like Melissa and her kind, he was simply blessed and he didn't have to settle for anyone who wasn't worthy of him.

She looked at herself in the mirror. Sheila Kingsly was worthy of him. The choice had been so simple, and she had made it so complicated. Story of her life.

That was it, then. The mask wasn't coming off. Let Melissa do whatever she wanted to Jack. He wasn't going to learn otherwise. Just like her mother had said—everyone had to look out for himself . . .

An idea came to her. If she was Melissa Antonelli, and she wanted to humiliate Jack Kidder, what location would she choose to do the deed? It would have to be at an event. Something big, like the final night of the masquerade.

Sheila could picture Melissa and her friends sitting around, planning something for Jack that would make the ending of "Carrie" look like a meaningless little prank. They'd spend the rest of the year talking about it, ridiculing Jack.

Sheila stopped herself. Why was she thinking of Melissa this way? *Melissa* had not been unkind to her. It had been Yvette.

That didn't matter. They were all the same. They all deserved to endure the same punishment.

It's not your problem, Sheila. You've chosen. Sheila Holland is history. You're Sheila Kingsly now.

Sure, but Jack was the only one who didn't turn against her. She owed him for that.

What was it Gwen had said? "If she hurts Jack, I'll kill her."

Her response had been, "I'll help."

Sheila allowed a ragged gasp to escape her. *That* might have been going a little too far. If only there was some way to warn Jack, but he wouldn't listen. He was too far gone.

Maybe she could do something to Melissa.

Memories of the boys in the courtyard running and screaming in terror flooded into Sheila's mind. She had known what frightened them and she had become that thing. Maybe there was a way of keeping Melissa from hurting Jack too badly. Something Ian had told her last night revealed at least one thing that frightened Melissa.

Smiling, Sheila realized that there may very well be a way of putting the fear of God, or, at least, the fear of Sheila Kingsly into the girl. Sheila flinched. That was the first time she had thought of herself with her new name. It had come so naturally that it had almost frightened her.

Not quite.

Sheila left the house, anxious to head off disaster for her friend Jack. She was also looking forward to having a little fun for herself.

Twenty

Melissa Antonelli was in her bedroom when she heard the scratching outside her door. It was a strange sound, the kind an animal might make.

Her family didn't have any pets.

Maybe it was rats.

The thought terrified her as much as the idea of having to face Michael Roca in that costume tonight. She knew it was just him, could smell the plastic, see the seams. That should have made being close to him in that suit easier to take. It didn't.

Now there was something scratching at her door and it wasn't going away. Melissa had just gotten out of the shower. She clutched her terrycloth robe close and called for her father. No response. Running to the window, she looked out and saw that her dad's car was gone. Her mom had said that they needed some things from the store. Apparently, they had gone out shopping.

The scratching grew more fierce.

Downstairs, in the kitchen, there would be some

kind of note. *Went out to pick up a few things, be back soon, sweetie!*

That didn't help her now. She was already running late. If she didn't hurry, Jack would be at the club before she was, and she didn't want him to think she was standing him up. This was going to be a special night for both of them.

The scratching stopped. Maybe it hadn't been at the door at all, she told herself. She lived in a big house and noises traveled in weird ways. It could have just been a squirrel or something on the roof, or in the attic.

Sure, it could have been, but what if it wasn't? What if it *was* a rat, a big one, too, and it was crouching down in front of the door, waiting for her to be stupid enough to let it inside?

Rats aren't that smart. No, but other creatures could be. It could be something a lot bigger, something smart enough to try and bait her. Fine. That was true. But what was she going to do, wait here all evening for her parents to get back home? She knew what her mother was like when she went shopping: *Just one more stop, just one more, that's all.* Then, five hours later, you get home.

Terrific. So she had to go out there at some point. It would be better to wait, she knew. Get dressed first. If she did that, however, the fear would become too much for her. The school psychologist, Ms. White, had told Melissa a thousand times that she had to learn to confront her fears right away. The longer she waited, the worse it became.

Melissa went to the door. She wondered what

Jack would have said, if he had been there. The answer to that was obvious. He wouldn't have *said* anything. He would go out there for her. Jack's courage astounded her. He wasn't afraid to act foolish in front of her, and he had been brave enough to risk rejection and ask her out tonight. Not that there was really any risk, but he didn't know that.

Well, she would show him that she was just as brave. She was bigger and tougher than anything that was out there. Just knowing how Jack felt about her gave Melissa the courage to face practically anything. She wasn't afraid.

Oh, that would be nice to believe.

Melissa went to her closet, pulled out the wooden bat she had been given during her first year with the girl's softball team, and walked to the door.

Deep breaths. You can do this, don't worry.

She yanked open the door. Nothing was there. She relaxed so totally that she nearly dropped the baseball bat. Then she saw the spot on the carpet. Charred black, a thin wisp of white smoke rising from it, as if acid had been splashed there. Reaching for the door, raising the baseball bat, Melissa knew it was too late. Something appeared in the doorway, something large and impossible. It shoved her back and walked into her bedroom.

Michael. It was him, in that stupid alien costume.

But it didn't smell like that. It smelled — different. Stank, actually. She couldn't see the seams on the reptilian costume, and the double jaws extended in ways that Michael's suit could not.

Either she had gone completely insane, or the thing in front of her was real.

Melissa swung the baseball bat. If this monster was real, then what she had just done was a crazy, futile gesture. But somehow she had to try and fight it.

The monster slapped at the baseball bat, shattering it. A hailstorm of wood fragments exploded in Melissa's face. She turned and tripped on the edge of her bed. Her head struck the carpeted floor.

This wasn't real, it couldn't be happening!

The nightmare became even worse as the creature reached down, gripped her shoulder, and turned her over, jamming its face in hers.

I can't pass out, she chanted in her head, *I can't let myself pass out. Even if none of this is real, even if I'm having a complete breakdown, I can't pass out!*

"Pretty, pretty, pretty," the monster said in a terrible voice.

Melissa felt a hot stinging sensation in her face and arms. She looked down and saw tiny splinters lodged in her flesh.

"Does the pretty pretty have plans for this evening?" the monster said in a taunting voice. Saliva dripped from the edge of its mouth. It struck the carpet beside her head and fizzed. She could feel the heat rise up next to her.

"Please—"

"Pretty please. The pretty pretty needs to say pretty please or else nothing happens."

Melissa started to cry. "Pretty please."

154

"Pretty please what?" the monster asked.

"Pretty please, don't kill me!"

The alien's head tilted to one side, like that of a wolf. "Why not? What has the pretty pretty got to offer?"

Michael, she thought. It's got to be Michael in costume. Only she knew that it wasn't. It was real and it was the most terrifying thing she had ever seen in her life.

"Anything, just don't kill me!" Melissa cried.

"What do we say?"

"Please! Pretty please!"

The monster's head swiveled from side to side. "I know what you could do. Stay home tonight. Keep away from the Kidder boy. If you do that, I'll let you live."

In her mind, Melissa was screaming, yes, yes, anything, but something prevented her from speaking those words. Jack meant something to her. She didn't want to hurt him.

"I don't hear the pretty pretty," the monster hissed. "Does she want a sweet? Sweets to the sweet. Perhaps a little kissy?"

The monster's center jaws extended, opened, and reached for Melissa's mouth. It's steaming, acid-like saliva bubbled and almost spilled on her face.

"No, don't! All right, I won't go!"

"And if he calls the pretty pretty?"

"I won't take the call."

"And when he comes to see the pretty pretty?"

"I won't be here."

"And when he comes up to you at school?"

"I won't talk to him."

The creature retracted its jaws and sprang back. "The pretty pretty is learning."

Rising to its impossible full height, its head grazing the ceiling, the monster turned and left without another word.

Sheila couldn't believe what she had just done. She had become herself again and had gone several blocks before she reached a convenience store. Ducking inside, Sheila went straight for the ladies' room, slammed the door behind herself, fell to her hands and knees, and threw up in the toilet.

Worshipping the porcelain god, she thought giddily. When she was done, she flushed the toilet, struggled to her feet, and washed her face. She had enjoyed that *far* too much. In the mirror, she saw her features shifting slightly. Then they molded firmly into the beautiful facade of Sheila Kingsly.

The mask's power was not infinite, she realized. If she tried something like that again without resting, both she and the mask would be in trouble. An odd sense of quiet came over her. The voice in her head, that of the mask, was stilled.

She used to read the Spider-Man comic strip in the newspaper. What was it they always said in that comic?

With great power comes great responsibility.

Tonight, she had been selfish and irresponsible. That she was even capable of what she had done frightened her immensely, but that fear paled beside her worry that if she did something like that again, she would not be able to stop herself.

What were those things she was saying? That wasn't her talking. It was the mask. Was that its true voice? Had she heard it clearly tonight for the very first time?

Sheila studied herself in the mirror. The paleness was retreating and her normal color was already coming back. In minutes, she would look completely normal again. The mask was taking care of her. It wouldn't do for her to show up at the final night of the masquerade looking like death, now would it?

Staring at the beautiful face in the mirror, Sheila wondered if she had ever seen anything so ugly in her entire life.

Twenty-one

Sheila arrived at the club wearing an outfit even more daring than the first one the mask had dreamed up for her. Her magnificent body was cloaked in a fishnet body stocking with strategically placed patches of soft black velour, black leather boots and gloves, and several bits of jewelry. Her hair was piled high and held in place by the mask's original tiara with its inverted looped cross and collection of miniature swords. The mask had also provided her with a strange facial design unlike any it had previously manifested.

Ian stared at her in shock. "You look unreal. Like someone just made you up."

"I can be anything you want me to be," she said, falling happily into his arms. She giggled as he caught her.

"Are you okay?"

Sheila laughed. "Fine."

Actually, she was more than "fine." Considerably more. She wondered if she appeared to be drunk or stoned. The mask had done something to her mind before she left the bathroom in the convenience store. A strange euphoric wave had washed over her as she had reached for the door. There were chemicals in the brain, substances the body released when it was enduring terrific pain. Endorphins, that was it. She felt as if she had been flooded with them and was absolutely flying.

"Why don't we sit down?" Ian asked.

"Okay," Sheila said, unable to stop giggling. They reached a booth and slid into it together.

"You want to tell me what's so funny?"

"Uh-uh," she said, "I wanna do *this*." Sheila launched herself at Ian, kissing him with a fiery intensity. They remained like that for several minutes, lost in the pleasure of their kisses, until someone cleared their throat. Ian broke from the kiss. Sheila moaned discontentedly. She had no intention of stopping.

Standing before them was Jenny Demos, the owner's daughter. She was an attractive blonde in her early twenties. "Sorry to interrupt. I was just wondering if you had seen Michael Roca?"

Ian shook his head.

"He was supposed to be master of ceremonies during the awards show. Frankly, I'm a little worried."

"Don't be. Michael wouldn't miss this."

"Okay," she said. "But if your friend doesn't show, I'm sticking *you* with the honor."

"You bet."

The woman looked at Sheila strangely then turned away. She produced an order pad and waited on a group of kids at a nearby table, occasionally stealing glances in Sheila's direction.

"I wonder what her problem is," Sheila said, her elation fading.

"Who knows and who cares? This is the big night," he said.

Sheila's smile faltered. "What do you mean?"

"You promised. Tonight you're going to tell me all about yourself."

"Oh that. Yeah, sure." Sheila nodded. "Right."

"You haven't changed your mind?"

"No," she said, a bit too quickly. "I haven't changed my mind."

"Good. 'Cause there's one thing I forgot to tell you the other night."

"What's that?"

"I hate mysteries and I want to know the real Sheila."

Sheila looked away and saw Jack for the first time. He sat alone, wearing his magician's costume. Melissa was nowhere in sight. Good.

"You know Yvette Depree?" Ian asked.

The name filled Sheila with loathing. "I know her."

"Her boyfriend was here before. He's telling everyone that he dumped Yvette, but I heard she broke up with him this morning."

"This morning," Sheila repeated dully. For some reason, that sounded wrong to her.

"Typical, y'know. He can't be the one who got dumped, he's got to have been the one who did the dumping."

"Yeah," Sheila said, slightly dazed. She felt as if some incredibly important bit of knowledge had grazed the surface of her consciousness, then retreated.

"Are you sure you're okay?"

Sheila shuddered. The fog enshrouding her thoughts was beginning to lift. "When was the last time you saw Michael?"

"In history class, this afternoon. Why?"

"No reason," Sheila said, but that was a lie. There was a reason, she just couldn't remember what it was. Certain things that had happened today were nagging at her, but she couldn't understand why she felt so troubled. Of course Michael and Yvette had been seen today. That was normal, why should it feel so wrong?

The confrontation with her mother played in her head. Something about it bothered Sheila. It was something obvious, something she should have been able to see, but was too blind to register. The thought came to her that maybe her lack of understanding was not her fault. It was possible that she was being *prevented* from seeing what had been wrong this afternoon.

She may want to be ignorant, and that may be making the force blocking her perceptions that much stronger. The desire to blindly follow where she was being led was no longer overwhelming. All her life, she had wanted to see the truth. That was why she had become a member of Freedom International. Closing your eyes to injustice was easy. Confronting evil was always more difficult. But there were people with hearts as black as pitch, and if the darkness was not confronted, it grew more and more powerful.

That was what Sheila wanted to do with her life. Confront injustice. Protect people who could not protect themselves. That's why she had run into the courtyard this afternoon.

She wondered why she had never been able to see that before. It was so simple, so painfully obvious—just like whatever had been wrong with her confrontation a few hours ago with her mother. That, however, she still could not see.

Sheila looked at Ian and wondered how he would react if she shared with him the thoughts that had been racing through her head. He wouldn't laugh, she knew that much. But would he *understand?* There was only one way to find out.

"Ian—"

She stopped as her gaze suddenly focused beyond Ian to Jack, who was returning to his table, his face white, his eyes filled with tears that he could not hide.

Oh God, she thought. He must have called Melissa to make sure that she was all right. She must have told him that she wasn't coming, that they were not going to see one another.

That was what she had wanted, of course. Jack would feel a little pain now, that was to be expected. But this way, he would be spared an even greater pain later.

Who in the hell gave you the right to make that decision, she screamed at herself within the confines of her thoughts.

Melissa was going to hurt him!

Maybe. But you made that a certainty.

"Sheila?" Ian asked.

"I've got to do something," she said. "I'll be right back."

Ian slid out of the booth first. Sheila brushed past him and went to Jack's table. He looked up at her and attempted to wipe away his tears. She saw that he had taken out an envelope filled with photographs and was staring at one of Melissa.

"She's not worth it," Sheila said.

Anger flared within her friend. "Who are you?"

"Can I sit down?"

Jack shrugged. Sheila pulled up a chair. Her friend was dejected.

"Believe me, whoever she is, she's not worth it. If she can't see how wonderful you are and how much you have to offer, then she's just not worth it."

"What's going on is that obvious, huh?" he asked, humiliated. "I should have just left."

"You didn't want to be alone. Now you're not alone. There's nothing wrong with that."

Jack ran his hand over his forehead. In the pulsing red and blue lights of the Night Owl Club, he looked more like a scarecrow than ever. Sheila noted that if she hadn't known him so well, his long, thin nose and crooked smile might have made him appear threatening. "Look, don't take this wrong, but I don't want your sympathy. You don't even know me, and you sure as hell don't know her."

"I know you a lot better than you think," Sheila said. This was amazing. She was feeling more in control of herself than she ever had when wearing the mask. As she had tortured Melissa, Sheila had felt like a far-away participant. Someone else had

163

been writing her lines. Now she was in control. Studying firsthand the damage she had brought about, Sheila felt horrible.

She reached for the envelope filled with photographs and saw that they were all taken at the masquerade. Suddenly she was reminded of photography club, and of the Monday deadline for the newspaper contest. Everything that had once been important to her had taken a backseat to her experiences with the mask. But it was those things that she had been denying that helped to define who she was. If she ignored everything that had been important to her as Sheila Holland, then she would no longer be her old self placed in a new, improved body. She would be someone else entirely.

Maybe that had been the point all along, she realized. Sheila spotted a photo of Ian and herself and withdrew it from the pack.

"I just got these developed tonight," Jack said. "I wanted to surprise Melissa with hers. They came out wonderful. Not really hard when you have someone like her for a subject."

Sheila raised the photo of Ian and herself and gasped.

"I sort of promised that one to someone. But, I dunno. You might as well take it. Something went wrong with this print, anyway. I got this like weird shadow, this double image."

The photo revealed Sheila, Ian, and a blur darting out from behind Sheila. Whatever it was, it moved as if to escape the bright light of the camera flash. Sheila stared at the image. It was a thing more shadow than light, a creature with glinting objects that could be razor blades for eyes, needles for a mouth, and scalpels for fingers.

Suddenly, Sheila *understood*.

When the mysterious girl had been in her room, she had seen this thing for the brief instant when she had turned on the lights. The face it had worn, the human face—*that* had been the illusion. This thing could make itself look like anything it wanted to look like.

Memories of the conversation with her mother returned again, but this time they were not clouded by the mask's efforts to deceive her. Sheila had put the mask on at lunchtime and had never taken it off. Her mother had seen Sheila wearing the mask and had spoken to the girl as if she were Sheila Holland, not Sheila Kingsly.

Colleen Holland had not been the person she had argued with this afternoon.

It had been this *thing*.

Jack looked up as Ian joined them. He touched Sheila's arm. She dropped the photograph then threw her arms around him, shaking uncontrollably.

"Honey, what's the matter?" he asked.

Another memory pierced her consciousness. *Michael Roca, staring at her face. "How did you find out about the Abassax? The patterns you're wearing. It's Egyptian. You know that, right?"*

No, she didn't know any such thing, but she would desperately like to find out before midnight and the arrival of the shadow creature.

"Do you know where Michael lives?" Sheila

asked.

"Sure, we hang out all the time."

"Take me there."

"Right now? Are you kidding?"

"No."

Ian frowned. He could tell from her expression that she was dead serious. "Let's go."

Sheila looked over to Jack. "Do you want to come with us?"

Jack seemed just as confused as Ian. Sheila wasn't exactly sure why she wanted Jack to come along, except that she had a feeling things were going to turn bad tonight, and she wanted someone who was a true friend of Sheila Holland at her side.

"Sure," he said, gathering up the photographs. "What else do I have to do?"

Together, they left the club.

Twenty-two

There were no lights on at Michael's house. Ian knocked at the front door while Jack went around to the rear. No one was home.

"I'm sorry, Sheila," Ian said. He was still wearing his space marine outfit and he felt a little silly being out in public this way. Sheila had reminded him that it was Halloween night. Nevertheless, standing before Michael Roca's house, Ian looked uncomfortable.

Jack emerged from the side of the house. "Nothing."

"We need to get inside. Even if that means breaking in."

"Huh?" Ian said. "Why should we do that? What's so important—"

"Don't ask me to explain, all right?" Sheila ran her hand over her face. The mask was tingling, as if it were attempting to punish her once again for this line of action, but it simply lacked the strength. "We just need to."

"I'm outta here," Jack said. "I'll walk home, thanks."

"No!" Sheila cried, running to him. She grabbed his arm. "You could get us in there. I know you can."

Jack frowned. "Just because my father's in jail for B & E doesn't mean I know how to pick locks. It's not something that runs in the genes."

"I know that. But I also know that you can do it. I've *seen* you do it."

Staring at Sheila in disbelief, Jack shook his head. Sheila bit her lip. Jack had only broken into a house once, and it had been as a favor to Sheila. Her parents were away for the weekend and she had locked herself out of the house.

"You couldn't have," he said.

Sheila hugged herself. She had been Sheila Holland when Jack had broken into her house, not Sheila Kingsly. She wondered if, on some unconscious or intuitive level, he knew that it was her. That could explain why he had been willing to follow Sheila Kingsly, a complete stranger. Or maybe he remembered what Ian had done for him that day in the auditorium and felt he owed the guy a favor.

Suddenly, there was a muffled crash. Sheila and Jack turned to see Ian standing beside a broken first floor window. He had picked up a rock, wrapped his jacket around his arm, and smashed the glass.

"I don't believe you just did that," Jack said.

Ian ignored Jack as he carefully reached inside, unlocked the window, and cleared it of glass fragments. He opened the window and turned to Sheila. "I don't know. I can't explain it. You make me crazy. I can't think when I'm around you. You wanted in, let's go in."

"This is a crime," Jack said. "A house this nice, they've probably got a silent alarm."

Sheila looked around. They were in an affluent neighborhood.

Ian shook his head. "They're getting one, they don't have it yet. Michael and I talked about it two days ago."

Bending low, Ian was about to force himself through the opening when Jack stopped him and said, "I'm smaller than you are. If there's still any glass, you'll get cut up. I can avoid it."

With a catlike ease, Jack crawled through the window, then came through the house to open the front door for Sheila and Ian.

"Where's Michael's room?" Sheila asked.

"Upstairs," Ian said.

"Take us up there."

Jack shook his head as he followed the other two up the stairs. "I don't believe we're doing this."

They reached Michael's room and went inside. Posters from gore films were everywhere, along with books, comics, and videos. Masks Michael had made were everywhere. Some were disgusting special effects models — a man with an axe sticking out of his head, a woman with her eyeball dangling by a loose thread of muscle — while others were very stylish. Some were like the mask Sheila had found at the antique barn.

"Just tell me what we're doing here," Ian said.

"Why couldn't this have waited until Michael showed up at the club? We probably just missed him."

"I don't think so," Sheila said, not yet understanding why she felt so confident of that fact. "Michael said something about the mask I'm wearing."

"You're not wearing a mask," Ian said.

"Well—the makeup. These designs on my face. They come from something called the Abassax. It's Egyptian. Michael knew all about it. I need to know everything he knew."

"He's got all these books on masks," Jack said. "Maybe he read about it in one of these."

"Okay, let's start there."

Flustered but compliant, Ian helped Sheila and Jack page through the various texts. She noticed the clock. Ten thirty. Only an hour and a half left. How had it gotten so late?

It took twenty-five minutes before Ian cried, "Got it!"

He had been sitting at Michael's desk and Sheila went to him. Jack leaped from the bed and crowded in behind.

"See? There are like three pages on this thing. Is that enough?"

"I don't know," Sheila said truthfully.

Ian was getting tense. "Someone's going to see the light on. Or the Rocas are going to come home. I don't want to spend the rest of my life explaining why I was busted for breaking and entering when I was seventeen. Let's take this thing and go."

Sheila looked at her watch. Five minutes to

eleven. "Just let me skim it real quick. We're out of here at eleven, one way or the other."

"All right, all right. Quick."

Sheila pulled the book close and began to read. "The Abassax is a legend from the time of the pharaohs. It concerns a girl named Kamilah, the eldest daughter of the *Khalid* house. Though she was the first born, she was not the favored daughter. That honor fell to her sister, Sabah. Kamilah was fat and ugly, a selfish, manipulative child. Sabah was thin and beautiful, a priceless treasure of radiance, obedience, and intelligence. Kamilah often attempted to do harm to her sister by way of committing terrible pranks and attempting to lay blame at the feet by her sister. But the truth was found out, and Kamilah was sent away to be reared privately in another land.

"On her sixteenth birthday, Kamilah was approached by Shandrezahr, an ambitious sorcerer. He proposed a means of gaining not only vengeance upon her parents and her sister, but also their wealth and power. Shandrezahr had fashioned an incredibly beautiful mask which he called the Abassax. One night he joked that the mask was named after a demon he had bound to it, a creature that had no choice but to serve the mask's owner.

"Kamilah didn't care about demons. All she wanted to know was the sorcerer's plan. Shandrezahr claimed that the wearer of the mask could transform themselves into a perfect duplicate of any man, woman, or beast they had ever known or could ever imagine. Kamilah wanted the mask. Her

171

dream, above all else, was to be beautiful. She wanted to be regarded in the same manner as her ravishing sister, Sabah.

" 'What must I do?' asked Kamilah. The sorcerer instructed her to return to her native land, gain a private audience with her father, mother, and sister, then murder all three. When they were dead, she was to set a fire to destroy the evidence of her foul deed, then wait for Shandrezahr to rescue her.

"He would pretend to be a humble merchant who had, coincidentally, appeared that day to hawk his wares to Ali Khalid, Kamilah's father. He would enter the flaming room and give Kamilah the mask. With it, she would transform into the perfect likeness of her hated sister, Sabah, and they would use his magic to escape.

"The only corpse that had to be made completely unrecognizable by the flames was that of her sister. Kamilah accepted the wizard's terms. Less than a month later, the horrible crime had been committed. Kamilah's mother, father, and sister had been slain, and she had assumed her beautiful sibling's face and form.

"As the only surviving member of the Khalid house, after the murderous attack by her sister which only she survived, Kamilah, posing as Sabah, inherited everything. As per her agreement with the sorcerer, she split her newfound wealth with the 'kindly merchant' who had 'saved her life.' Shandrezahr took his newfound wealth and was never seen again.

"Kamilah lived the life she had dreamed of attaining since childhood. She had the love of the people, friends, and countless lovers. Over the decades, her beauty did not wither. Age did not touch her. Rumors began to spread. Kamilah was in league with the dark gods. She had entered a pact with them to forever preserve her beauty. Kamilah heard these wild tales and knew the time to act had arrived.

"One month later, Kamilah was dead. A terrible fire had left her corpse ravaged beyond recognition. Her story was ended, or so the world believed. The assets of her estate, surprisingly, were few. One of her servants, a young woman who later told the tale to scribes, gave one possible explanation: Kamilah had not died. She had murdered a girl she had taken from the streets and set the fire to cover her departure.

"The bulk of her wealth had been quietly removed over the course of several years. This was part of a contingency plan she had come up with years earlier, when she first realized that the mask would keep her young and beautiful for much longer than any human had a right to exist. The servant revealed that she had learned much of her mistress' plans one night when she had been trapped in Kamilah's bedchambers. The girl had been admiring Kamilah's private collection of sculptures and knew that she had to hide herself away when she heard Kamilah approaching. The penalty for being in Kamilah's bedchambers when the woman was not there was death.

"The servant claimed that Kamilah boasted of her powers and her wicked beginnings to a lover. Then, after she had taken what pleasure he had to give, she had walked away from the bed and allowed a terrible creature that seemed to manifest from the shadows to kill her partner. The monster consumed her lover's beauty and gave it to the mask's owner. At least one man died in this manner each year that the servant worked for her mistress. The servant was found horribly murdered a month after telling her tale.

"Throughout the years, the Abassax has cropped up, always in connection with men and women of great power. In the background of each of these persons lay mysterious deaths and disappearances, for it was said that the blood of three beautiful people was required to bind the Abassax to a new owner. More blood was needed throughout the decades to maintain the gift of beauty the mask bestowed."

Sheila pushed the book away with trembling hands and reached up to claw at the sides of the mask. She knew that everything she had just read was the truth. Images of Yvette Depree and Michael Roca sprang into her mind. She saw them crying and screaming as they were slowly ripped to pieces by the shadow creature. The monster was clever. It had hidden their bodies well, then spent time making brief appearances as both Yvette and Michael to keep any suspicions from being raised.

Her hands ran along the baseline of her jaw as she anxiously sought the edges of the mask. They no longer existed. Sheila began to scream and Ian tried to hold her. She shrugged him off, then rose, and looked at herself in the mirror.

She had made her choice. The mask was a part

of her now. God help her, it could not be removed.

The blood of three *beautiful people was required to bind the Abassax to a new owner.*

Three people. Yvette and Michael only made two. Maybe there was still time. If she could find the shadowman's final victim, maybe she could still escape a lifetime imprisoned to the mask.

The voice she had been listening to in her mind must have been that of Kamilah. The witch had freed herself from the bonds of the flesh by joining her soul to the mask. Either by midnight, or by the time the shadowman made his third kill, Sheila would cease to exist in any form, and Kamilah would live again.

It was crazy, but it was the only explanation that made sense to her. Sheila looked at the clock. It was a few minutes after eleven. She had less than an hour to live.

"Sheila, what's wrong?" Ian demanded. Behind him, Jack echoed his words. She ignored both of them.

Who would the shadowman have chosen? Then it came to her. The creature had not been the one making the choices. That had been Sheila's doing. She had loathed Yvette for stealing the spotlight from her and she had wanted the girl punished. The mask had tricked her into targeting Michael when his words caused the mask worry. It gave her agony, and she blamed Michael. She wanted him gone forever. The shadowman had granted both her wishes.

Now there was only one more kill required, and Sheila knew that it could only be one person. She turned to face Ian and Jack. "We have to get out of here and we have to get to Melissa."

They looked to one another in confusion.

"We have to do it *now!*"

Twenty-three

Sheila felt an oppressive wave of guilt and fear wash over her as they pulled up to Melissa's house. She knew that her primary concern should be the innocent girl who was being stalked by the mask's servant, but it was difficult not to think of what it would mean for her if the shadowman claimed the final victim. Only a few hours ago, the idea of being locked forever in the face and form of Sheila Kingsly had seemed like the fulfillment of all her dreams. Now it was a nightmare.

She had fidgeted with the edges of the mask on the drive, but she could not find them. The mask had grafted itself to her flesh completely. Did that mean that Melissa was dead already? They should have called her first, warned her to get out of her house, but where could they have told her to go? No matter where she ran, the shadowman would find her. So long as there was darkness, it could manifest.

In the last few moments, the entity within the

mask had risen from its slumber. The voice inside Sheila's head railed against her for her current course of action, promising that she would suffer punishments undreamt of if she did not stop immediately. Sheila ignored the voice and the lancing strikes of agony the mask sent into her flesh. The physical attacks were not that bad when compared with the mask's earlier assaults. Sheila decided that if she and the mask were truly joined, then it could not hurt her without hurting itself.

Go on then, the mask whispered in her head. *Go on and find all the sorrows you'll need for a lifetime of regret. You'll still have me. I'll never leave you, Sheila. We're one now. You have to trust me. I won't hurt you.*

Lies, Sheila thought. Lies meant to frighten her into submission. Images from videos regarding prisoners of conscience surfaced in her mind. She knew that sometimes a tormentor would assume a pleasing face or pretend to be an ally. That's all the mask was doing now.

Jack bolted out of the car the moment they came to a stop. Sheila tore open her door and launched herself after him. Ian was faster. He had the car in park and was out of the car instantly. In a blur he passed Sheila and caught Jack, grabbing him and clamping his hand over Jack's mouth before the boy could call out.

"Wait," Sheila said. "Listen. See those lights downstairs? Her parents are still up."

Movement came from a window upstairs. Someone had walked across the room. Sheila knew from her earlier visit that it was Melissa's bedroom window. She wondered if it had been Melissa or the shadowman moving around up there. How would they know? It could kill Melissa and assume her form.

"Jack, if you start screaming for her now, her parents are going to come and get in the middle of this. They probably won't let us see her, and we *have* to see her. Alone. Do you understand?"

Jack's body relaxed. Sheila looked to Ian and nodded. He released Jack.

"So what do you want to do? Break in through the back door and sneak in without anybody noticing?" Jack asked sarcastically.

"Yes, that's exactly what I want to do," Sheila answered.

Melissa had finally gotten dressed an hour earlier. When her parents arrived home, she ran into her father's arms. He asked her what was wrong and she didn't know what to tell him. Someone — no, some *thing* — had been in her room and it had told her not to go to the masquerade with Jack? He would rush her to the hospital, convinced that his daughter had been the victim of a violent attack. The doctors would cross their arms and say that she had invented these more fanciful memories of a giant creature from the movies coming after her to replace her real memories of a human attacker. Melissa had seen enough TV movies to know that they always came up with ways to rationalize the impossible.

The splinters in her skin, the bleeding, that had been real enough to cause genuine concern. Melissa said that she had been asleep and she woke up convinced there was a rat outside her door. She had opened the door and swung without looking. The bat had struck the jamb and splintered. They believed that one. She said that she was embarrassed, it was obviously part of a bad dream she had been having. They smiled, tended to her cuts, and were extremely kind.

She knew the truth. That was enough. Something had been in her house and it had not been Michael Roca in a costume.

"Melissa?"

She spun, startled to see the boy she had just been thinking about standing before her in her bedroom. Melissa took a step back and nearly lost her balance on the side of the bed. The TV on her dresser was turned on. She had been watching the news.

"Didn't you hear me come in?" Michael asked, his eyes wide and filled with an unspoken apology.

Melissa shook her head.

"Your parents let me in. Everyone was worried when you didn't show up tonight. I was, too."

She looked to the door. It was still closed. Considering how jumpy she was tonight, there was no way it could have been opened and shut again without her hearing it. Melissa opened her mouth to call out to her parents and suddenly Michael was beside her, inches from her.

"No, don't disturb them," he said. "I want to

talk with you privately. Is that all right?"

Chest heaving in fright, Melissa nodded. She wondered if she would be able to scream before Michael closed his hand over her mouth.

"Good," Michael whispered, pulling back his lips in a terrible smile. "*Very* good."

Sheila, Jack, and Ian were on the stairs, moving slowly, worried that a telltale creak would sound at any moment. At the head of the stairs, Sheila heard voices. A boy and a girl, talking. Without hesitation, she raced to Melissa's door and ripped it open. Inside, Melissa had been pressed up into a corner by Michael Roca. He turned to look at Sheila with a grin. Instead of teeth, he had glistening needles in his mouth.

"Get away from her!" Sheila cried.

Michael closed his mouth and backed away as Ian and Jack caught up with Sheila.

"Michael?" Ian asked.

"No, it's not Michael," Sheila said.

The dark-haired boy standing beside Melissa smiled once more. This time, his teeth were normal. Sheila had been the only one to see him for what he truly was.

"Of course it's me," he said, hands outstretched, palms up. "Who else would it be?"

Beside Michael, Melissa took one look at Jack and nearly burst into tears. Her sorrow over what she had done was enough to make her go forward. More than anything, she wanted to feel his arms around her.

Michael's arm shot out, stopping her. "Hold on."

Ian seemed confused. "What are you doing here?"

"A little of this, a little of that. No big deal, right? Everyone can just go home, the situation's under control." He giggled. Michael's words sounded as if they had been lifted from an episode of "Rescue 911."

Melissa's gaze was riveted on Jack's. "I'm sorry."

An idea seemed to strike Jack. "Did he make you say those things?"

"Not him," she whispered. "Someone—" She bit off her words as she saw Michael's malevolent stare.

Jack walked forward, anxious to take Melissa's hand and get her away from Michael, but Sheila stopped him.

"It's not safe. He *isn't* Michael."

"That's crazy," Michael said. "Come on, Ian. We've known each other all our lives. It's me, isn't it?"

Ian did not look convinced, but, apparently, no other explanation made sense to him. "Sure. 'Course it is. But what are you doing here?"

"I could ask the same thing," Michael said.

Melissa shuddered. Michael had not lowered his arm, and, for some reason, she was terrified by the very idea of touching his flesh to make him move.

No one spoke. For a few, brief seconds, the only sound in the room was the newscaster droning on and on.

"This just in," the immaculately groomed announcer said, lowering his tone to show his forced sincerity, "two bodies were found tonight in Cooper Hollow."

"Turn that off!" Michael snarled.

"No, leave it," Sheila said with a growing sense of finality.

Michael abandoned Melissa and walked over the top of the bed, dropping down on the other side and reaching for the TV's off button. He moved as quietly as a shadow. Behind him, Jack and Melissa ran to each other. Sheila watched as they grabbed each other with a fierceness that erased all doubts in her mind of Melissa's sincerity. She truly cared for Jack. Sheila could see that now.

Ian was on Michael before the machine could be shut off, knocking Michael's hand away from the television's control panel. The announcer went on. "The parents have identified the bodies as two local seventeen-year-olds, Yvette Depree and Michael Roca—"

With an angry shout, Michael struck Ian in the face, sending him flailing backward. Ian crashed against a dresser, breathing hard, but did not fall. "What the hell *is* this, Michael?"

The dark-haired boy shrugged. The television announcer had gone on to deliver a more upbeat piece to close the show. It was close to eleven-thirty. Michael turned off the set.

"This is unpleasantness," Michael said. "This can be avoided. Sheila, you know what's going on here. Now take your friends and get out before things get bloodier than they really have to."

"No," Sheila said.

Ian shook his head. "Michael—"

The dark-haired boy began to cackle insanely.

"Stop it," Sheila said softly. Michael continued to laugh. It was incredibly unnerving. *"Stop!"*

He stopped. A mock sadness crept across his movie-star features. "Before midnight. The traditional hour for masks to fall. I suppose we can defy convention and do things a little earlier, if you really want. Shall I show them?"

Sheila shuddered. "I want you to go away."

"Not likely."

The passage from Michael's book came to her. "Whoever wears the mask commands you."

The giggles came again. "You don't wear the mask. The mask wears you."

Sheila watched the creature wearing Michael's flesh with mounting fear.

"Let me show you something," the shadowman said as he began to tug at the skin of his face, "let me show *all* of you something very, very special . . ."

184

Twenty-four

Not one of them fainted as the shadowman revealed itself. That in itself was a triumph. The creature smiled as it unfurled the scalpels that served as its fingers. The razors that were its eyes glinted, as did the needles that were its mouth.

Melissa opened her mouth as if to scream. The shadowman was upon her, forcing its knife-like fingers against the underside of her chin. Jack tried to pull her away and the shadowman slapped him. Before either Sheila or Ian could catch him, Jack fell to the floor, striking his head on the side of a dresser. Sheila bent low next to him. He was bruised and bloody, but he was still breathing.

"*Hush-hush-hush-hush-hush,*" the shadowman whispered to Melissa, who regarded the creature with impossibly wide eyes. "*Scream and I'll join with the shadows, kill your parents, then return within seconds. I can do that, you know. I can do* anything. *Just ask your friend, Sheila.*"

"Get away from her," Sheila cried. "Please!"

"You chose this, Sheila. I gave you a chance for the others to be spared. I cannot extend that offer again. They've seen me. They know the truth."

"No one would ever believe them. Please," she begged. "Just don't hurt them and I'll do whatever you want."

"Isn't that generous?" the shadowman asked of no one in particular.

"Everything in that story was true," Ian said.

"More or less." The shadowman looked at Sheila. *"I've dispensed with my mask. Care to drop yours?"*

"I can't," she whispered.

The shadowman laughed. *"No, you can't, can you? Poor Sheila. You haven't the strength. No matter. Now they all have to die. You could have spared them. You chose not to. Greedy Sheila. Your greed will bring you and those you love terrible agony. All of it could have been avoided."*

No one moved for many seconds. Each feared that the shadowman would drive his sharp fingers through Melissa's flesh before they could stop the monster.

"I don't want to die," Melissa whispered.

"No, they never do," the shadowman said sadly. *"And that's a shame. Do you know why?"*

"Stop it," Sheila commanded, but the shadowman ignored her.

The creature turned back to Melissa. *"Let me tell you about the future. It's not a kind place."*

186

"You killed Michael and Yvette," Sheila hissed.

"I liberated them. Each was beautiful in their way. But the future would have been cruel. Yvette's beauty would have faded so quickly. If events had not been mercifully altered, she would have fallen in with a terrible man who would have helped her to become addicted to substances that make anyone old before his time. He would have beaten her, raped her, and she would have died giving birth to a deformed infant. With me, she suffered not at all. I have preserved her beauty.

"Michael, in one short week, would have fallen victim to an accident in his garage. A propane tank he was using was defective. Flames would have seared away his face. He would have survived for six horrible days in mind-numbing agony. My way, at least, his beauty has been preserved forever.

"And that brings me to you, dear Melissa. Would you care to know the horrors that await you should you live to see the dawn? I can tell them to you. I'm magic. I can see the future. I can—"

"Yes," Melissa whispered, mesmerized, "tell me."

"No!" Sheila screamed. "It's a lie. Everything he says is a lie!"

"Quiet, pretty Sheila. It will be much easier on your friend if she chooses her fate."

"Like I chose this?" Sheila asked, her hand curling against her chest.

"You did."

"You lied to me. You told me everything I wanted to hear."

"You listened."

The glazed look left Melissa's eyes. The shadowman turned back to her, angry. Sheila realized that the creature was not as strong as it had been. Why hadn't it just killed Melissa and the others by now? There was nothing any of them could do to stop it.

A passage from the story she had read in Michael's book came to her: The mask feeds on beauty. It derives its strength from defiling beauty. There was nothing less attractive in the world than what fear could do to a person.

It was feeding *off* the fear it inspired!

Sheila wondered how this knowledge might help her to save herself and her friends. If there was nothing more ugly than fear, then there was certainly nothing more beautiful than love. What was the first thing the shadowman had done? It had knocked out Jack. The love Jack held for Melissa must have been blinding to the creature, a light it had to put out.

"Beauty has its dark side," the shadowman whispered. *"Shadows and light. That has always been the case. And no service is provided free, Sheila. Now let me get on with it."*

Sheila straightened slightly. The creature was asking her permission. It needed her leave. How had the shadowman responded when Sheila said that she could not remove the mask?

You haven't the strength.

"No. I'm not letting you do anything else."

The shadowman trembled with rage. *"You don't seem to understand what waits in the future for you if this child lives past midnight. I'll show you."* Suddenly, the shadowman regained the guise of the beautiful young woman who had appeared in Sheila's room last night. *"Sheila, this is Sarah Jennings. You wondered before where the name came from. She owned the mask before you."*

The monster transformed again, this time into the image of the television newscaster whose image had flickered on the small set on the dresser just a few minutes ago. *"Would you like to see what became of her when she tried to defy the mask?"*

The newscaster's features melted into those of Sarah Jennings. Sheila watched as Sarah aged at an incredible rate, her flesh shrinking and growing tight on the bone, until she was little more than a zombie-like, withered husk.

"She was forced to live like this for almost a week before the mask allowed her to kill herself."

The shadowman became the newscaster once more. *"Sarah was found like that by her boyfriend, who said that one week earlier she looked perfectly healthy. Doctors were at a loss to explain the strange disease that had caused her to age so rapidly. Sarah Jennings was nineteen years-old at the time of her death."*

Once again, the shadowman assumed its true, nightmarish appearance. *"That could be you, Sheila. How about it? You can die horribly, or you can give some sweets to the sweet!"*

The monster was gearing up for its kill. If she was going to act, she had to do it now. An idea came to her.

Sheila could transform. Become anyone. But all those other forms were beautiful. Hers was not.

The words of her teacher, Mrs. Lang, came back to her: Beauty comes from within.

But she had become ugly on the inside, too. She had allowed two people to die.

Yes, the voice of the mask said frantically, *that's true. It was your hatred. Your desire to be rid of them. That was all that was needed. Once you had chosen, the rest was easy. Now choose one last time. Choose and I can make everything right again! I'll spare Ian. Anything you want. But give Melissa to me! I need her so I can live again!*

No, Sheila thought. It was not her fault that Yvette and Michael were dead. She had not commanded the shadowman to kill. The mask had been using her, preying upon her weakness.

No more.

Sheila suddenly became aware that Ian was staring gape-mouthed at her. She could feel the flesh of her face bubble and transform. The shadowman watched her solemnly, its scalpel-like fingers edging ever so slightly from Melissa's flesh. On the floor, Jack began to stir. He watched as Sheila's body began to change.

It's too late for that, the voice of the mask screamed. *Too late for me to be rid of you, too late for you to be rid of me. Cooperate or you'll suffer the way Sarah suffered!*

Sheila ignored the voice in her head. Finally, the shape settled, and, in the mirror lining the wall, Sheila saw that the mask had taken on the image of her true face. She took Ian's hands.

"This is who I am. Sheila Holland. I'm not rich. I'm not beautiful. I'm not real proud of the things I've done. But this is who I am on the inside. This is the only person I can ever be. The only person I ever *want* to be. I don't know if you can love me like this. I don't know if you'll ever be able to forgive me for lying to you, for making up Sheila Kingsly, and for never telling you about myself. I don't know, Ian. And don't take this wrong, but I don't care.

"I love you, and I'd give almost anything to have a life with you. But I'm not willing to give up someone else's life for it. I don't have the right to make that kind of decision.

"I don't know what's going to happen to me now. I just want you to know how much I love you and how sorry I am."

His grip tightened on her hands.

"Can you love me, anyway?"

"I don't know," he whispered.

"Then I'll just have to live with that," Sheila said.

Deep inside Sheila's mind, she heard a terrible scream. Pain unlike any she had felt before surged through her, and the room was engulfed in a blinding light. The light faded and she heard a thud. She glanced down to see the mask lying on the floor, rocking back and forth.

191

It was ugly and decrepit, just as her mother had said. She had never been able to see its corruption until this very moment.

Sheila looked to the mirror, terrified that her true face had been ravaged by the mask as one last parting gift.

Instead, she saw the face she had been born with. For the first time in her life, she was truly grateful to see that face. She smiled and a spark of understanding came to her.

"Damn," she whispered. "I really am beautiful."

She turned and saw that the shadowman was gone. Jack had risen on uncertain legs and had taken Melissa in his arms. Ian stared at Sheila in shock. She wanted to say something to him. Anything. But all she could do was turn down her eyes in shame.

When she looked up again, the door was open and he was gone.

Epilogue

Weeks passed and Sheila did not receive so much as a phone call from Ian. The romance between Jack and Melissa blossomed. They were inseparable. Sheila still felt pangs of jealousy toward Melissa—after all, the girl had taken her best friend away from her. But she managed to keep a tight rein on those emotions. The important thing was that Jack was happy. Since Sheila had confessed the terrible act she had committed upon Melissa in disguise, the beautiful young woman had been unable to look at Sheila the same way again. Sheila was fairly certain that Melissa was not going to tell Jack. She wanted to forget that it had happened. That was the other reason for Sheila's reticence to approach Jack and Melissa as a couple. She knew that it would be a long time, if ever, until Melissa found it in herself to forgive Sheila and put what happened in the past.

Sheila had taken a part-time job at a one stop shopping center in Wakefield. Her relationship with her mother had been steadily improving, and she was happy to see that her parents, on the few occasions when they got together, were no longer fighting. They knew that all they could do was try to work together to repair their marriage. Sheila held out little hope, but it was good to see them getting along better.

Gwen apologized to Sheila and they spent more time together than ever before, but somehow it just wasn't the same. Sheila Kingsly was gone, but she had left a mark upon Sheila Holland. It was not a bad thing. If anything, she was stronger now than she had ever been.

It was that strength that allowed her to drive to Ian's house on a Saturday in November, park down the street, and begin the walk back. She had heard around school that Ian was having a party that afternoon. A cook-out. The same one that had been scheduled for Halloween weekend, then canceled because of Yvette's and Michael's funerals. Sheila had not been invited, but she doubted that anyone would stop her.

The day was unusually warm, and all she needed was a sweater. The afternoon sun burned in her eyes as she walked past the line of cars to the Montgomery home. The music and laughter could be heard from a block away. Finally, she emerged at the back of the house, where the party was in full swing.

Ian was standing by the grill wearing an apron that read "Spatula Man!" and he was busy with a full plate of meats. He was smiling, happy. That was good, Sheila thought, and almost turned and ran.

"Special recipe, special recipe, you ain't gonna get it this good at McDoogals or any of those places!" Ian cried, sounding like a carnival hawker.

Taking a deep breath, Sheila carved a path through the partying teenagers and stopped when she was directly across the grill from Ian. He took one look at her and his smile faded.

"Hi," she said.

"Hi, yourself." He looked down at the meats he was preparing. They sizzled and spat as he flipped them over.

"I just thought maybe we should talk," Sheila said.

Ian's shoulders sank. "Why? What do you have to say to me that I would possibly want to hear?"

Sheila winced. She thought she would be prepared for his anger, but this was worse than she had pictured. The flatness of his tone, the coldness in his eyes—it was almost too much to take.

"You have every right to be mad at me," Sheila said.

"Furious."

She nodded. "Furious, okay."

A ragged breath escaped Ian as he looked up and met her gaze. "Just tell me one thing."

"What's that?"

"Tell me what you did with it."

"Yeah," Sheila said. She figured he would want to know that. "After you left, the three of us took the mask down to the city dump in Wakefield. There was a fire in the furnace. We tried to throw it in and burn it, but it wouldn't burn. None of us wanted to touch it. Melissa took these salad tongs from the kitchen. We used those. It was really pretty silly, I suppose. When you think about it."

"What did you *do* with it?"

"The only thing we could think to do was wrap it up in blankets, tie a whole bunch of bricks to it, then throw it off the Wakefield Bridge."

"Did it come back up?"

"No."

"That doesn't mean anything, you know."

"I know."

"It could still come back. That thing could still get it out of the water and give the mask to someone else."

"What did you want me to do?" she shouted. "We tried to get rid of it. We did the best job we could, all right?"

Ian looked down. "Damn!"

Two of his steaks were burning. He yanked

the meats from the grill, hurled them to the ground, then stalked off. Sheila ran to follow him.

"You tell me something!" she cried as his long strides kept him well ahead of her. He was walking away from the crowd of teenagers, toward the woods. "You tell me that all you cared about was what that mask showed you, that all you wanted was to get your hands on Sheila Kingsly and you didn't feel anything for me beyond that. You tell me that, Ian, and I'm gone, I'm history!"

He stopped and turned. "That's all I felt."

Sheila shuddered. "Then maybe you weren't worth loving."

Her heart heavier than it had ever been, Sheila turned and walked back to the party. She heard a sound behind her. Running footsteps. Then a hand on her shoulder, spinning her around. She was crying. Damn it.

"What?" she asked as she looked into Ian's face. "You want to hurt me a little more? You want to humiliate me a little more? Fine, go ahead. I deserve it."

"No, I, uh—I lied. I wanted to hurt you, I was mad, so I lied."

"Okay," she said, flinching as he stepped forward and gently wiped the tears from her eyes.

"I don't know what I feel, to be honest. There's something I felt when I looked at you the other way that I still feel. I don't understand it. I don't know what it is. All I know is that it's there. That's all I can tell you, that's all I can offer."

"Yeah," Sheila said, trembling like a little kid.

"I thought for a while that the mask had made me feel like this toward you. I thought I had just been manipulated. I don't know—I don't think that now. Standing here this close to you, it just doesn't seem right."

"What doesn't seem right?" she asked, somehow producing a smile. "Standing here this close to me? Is that what you're saying?"

"No. You know it isn't."

They stared at each other. Sheila spoke first. "Teasing. So what do we do now?"

"I don't know. Why don't we try to start over?"

"Okay."

He held out his hand. "Ian Montgomery."

She took it, using her free hand to wipe away more tears. "I know."

"You're still crying," he said.

"Happy tears. It's good."

"Go on."

"Sheila," she said. "Sheila Holland."

"So what's important to Sheila Holland? What does she care about? What does she believe in? I knew this other girl named Sheila. She'd never answer me when I asked her those questions."

"She wouldn't?" she asked, amazed at the tentative, but playful lilt in her voice.

"Uh-uh."

"Probably gave you some kind of crap about being a woman of mystery."

"Yeah."

"You seem like the type who would hate mysteries."

"You got it."

She laughed. "Okay. So what's important to me. Um, I like photography. Jack won the contest, you know."

"That's good."

"I didn't even end up entering. I just didn't, you know, have time. I had other things going on."

"Sure."

"Uh—I want to help people. Ever hear of an organization called Freedom International?"

Smiling, Ian took out his wallet, withdrew a card, and handed it to Sheila. It was identical to the one in her purse. The logo for Freedom International was emblazoned at the top.

"I see this, um, mystery stuff kind of goes both ways, doesn't it?"

"Yeah, it does," he said as he put the card away. "You hungry? I make the best burgers in the state."

"Yeah, sure."

"It's true," he said as he turned and led her back in the direction of the grill.

"Prove it."

"Might take some time. We'd probably have to drive around to every burger joint in New York, you know, taste test, compare. It could take years."

Sheila covered her face. The tears were back. She laughed and it sounded funny to her. She was trembling as she felt Ian take her hand. "I'm up for it."

"Yeah, you know what?" he asked.

"What?"

"Me, too."

They walked back to the party, ignoring the looks and the whispers, lost to everyone and everything but each other.

About the Author

NICK BARON grew up in a small New England town not unlike Cooper Hollow, the fictional setting for the Nightmare Club series. His memories of living in Cooper Hollow's uncanny twin continue to inspire him. His hometown, like Cooper Hollow and every small town, had its dark side.

Nick now lives in Florida, where he writes horror and fantasy novels under another name. As a writer, his earliest influences were authors such as Ray Bradbury, Harlan Ellison, Stephen King, and Dean Koontz. Nick believes these writers stretched the boundaries of imagination and terror without losing the humanity and humor that people find within themselves in even the most chilling circumstances.

The author loves movies and has worked in television as a writer and director. Currently he is working on several new projects, including more books in *The Nightmare Club* series.

Nick likes to hear from readers. He, and everyone at *The Nightmare Club,* would enjoy knowing how you like the books, and what you'd like to read in future stories. Write to him c/o The Nightmare Club, Zebra Books, 475 Park Avenue South, New York, NY, 10016. If you would like a reply, please include a stamped, self-addressed envelope.

SNEAK PREVIEW!

Here is a special preview of the next *Nightmare Club*. *The Room* by Vincent Courtney, ·on sale in October 1993.

THE NIGHTMARE CLUB #5
THE ROOM
Vincent Courtney

Bone Fenimore saw his victim standing at the locker down the hall. He ducked behind a corner in the science building at Cooper High and waited. The shiny metal hook in his hand felt slippery from his sweaty fingertips. A girl, Mary Kelly, walked by him and stared. He blew a kiss at her and she rolled her eyes and went down the hall. Bone focused his attention back to Alvin Merritt, his intended victim. Alvin was the star fullback for the Cooper High football team. He was also a braggart and picked on Bone unmercifully. Now at the right moment, the skinny Fenimore would have his revenge.

Alvin closed his locker and clamped the lock

shut. He started walking toward the corner where Bone was waiting.

Bone smiled as his victim approached.

Alvin strutted down the hall with the arrogance of a pampered athlete.

"Come on, big shot," Bone said to himself as he got the hook ready to strike.

Alvin kept coming.

"Come on."

Alvin stopped for a moment and looked to his left.

Bone tensed. Had he been seen?

The big fullback reached into his back pocket and pulled out his comb. He combed his hair while he looked at his reflection in the window of Mrs. Horst's room.

Bone sighed.

Alvin put the comb back into his pocket and started down the hall again.

"What's up, Truck?" he said when he saw his buddy, Mark Calhoun, a tackle on the team, sitting on a bench about fifty feet away.

"You, Bull," a smiling Mark said pointing at his friend.

Alvin waved and walked past the spot where Bone Fenimore was waiting.

Bone readied the hook. He took a quick breath and made his move.

It was over in a second.

"Hey, watch it, dweeb," Alvin said as Bone bumped into him and the hook found its mark.

"Sorry," Bone said in his best apologetic voice.

"Next time, I'll knock you on your scrawny ass."

"Right," Bone said, trying to contain his grin as he watched the big man on campus and football star walk away with a two-foot yellow tail with purple polka dots hanging from his belt loop by the paperclip hook Bone had fashioned.

Jennifer Struthers giggled as Merritt strutted by her. Her friends, Eva van Hudmon and Susan Buren, joined her. Across the hall, Tony Sims, Bone's best friend, smiled and shook his head as he looked at the colorful tail streaming in the cool November wind and then over at his friend. Bone gave him a thumbs-up signal and Tony shook his head to indicate what he thought of hanging a tail on one of the toughest guys in school. He couldn't believe the lengths that Bone went to sometimes just to get a laugh.

Antagonizing Alvin Merritt wasn't the brightest thing you could do under the best of circumstances, but when you weighed in at a hundred and thirty pounds and couldn't fight your way out of a wet paper lunch sack like Bone, it bordered on insanity. But Tony had to admit that it was pretty hilarious to see the cocky football stud strutting down the hall trailing a yellow tail with purple polka dots. And the laughing, chuckling, giggling students Merritt left in his wake apparently agreed.

Bone ran over to where Tony was standing.

"Look at the rare specimen of a Bull with a polka dot tail. Pretty impressive, eh?"

"It'll be impressive when Alvin makes you eat that thing."

"I took care of that possibility by making the tail out of rice paper," Bone said smiling. "If rice's good for the Chinese it's good for me."

Tony fought back a grin. "What about the paperclip?"

"No prob. Full of iron."

Tony laughed and shook his head. "You finish your Spanish homework?"

"*Sí, sí, señor.* Mucho finisho."

"Let me see it for a sec.

"Oh, no *señor,* that would be cheating."

"I just want to see the verb tenses."

"Okay, but it will cost you some pesos."

"Just give it to me, Fenimore."

Bone reached into his folder and pulled out his Spanish homework. He handed it to his friend.

As Tony checked his answers against his friend's, Bone asked him, "So are we going to the Night Owl Club tonight?"

"Are you sure this is right?" Tony said pointing at one of the answers.

"Yeah, I'm sure. So are we going?"

"If my aunt is feeling okay, but I don't

know." Tony looked at the answer again. "You sure about number three? It doesn't look right."

"Man, who has the A in Spanish and who's barely pulling a C?"

"Chill out, so it's right," Tony said as he checked his other answers, changing the wrong ones to the right ones.

"I hope Cindy's gonna be there tonight," Bone said, picturing the pretty blond girl who sat in front of him in math class. Cindy Macleod was Pam Williams' best friend and Pam was Tony's steady squeeze.

Tony looked up from the homework paper. "Why? Every time she's hanging with us, you don't ask her to dance or try to make a move on her."

"She likes Kevin."

"Just because they were dancing at the masquerade together last week doesn't mean they're dating."

"How do you know?"

"Pam told me, you dork. How else would I know?"

Bone shrugged as the warning bell rang for third period.

"Well, I better get my butt in gear. I have to go all the way to the gym," Tony said as he handed Bone his Spanish homework and headed down the hallway.

"See you at lunch," Bone said.

Tony walked backward as he spoke, "I'm going home at noon. I have to drive my aunt to the doctor. It's Friday check-up time."

"Oh, okay, so call me this afternoon about hitting it tonight."

"Yeah," Tony shouted as he turned around and hustled toward the gymnasium.

Bone started to head for his English class when he discovered that he had left his English book in his locker. "Damn," he said under his breath as he ran to the locker to get his book.

As he approached the locker and saw something hanging from his lock, a sick lumpy worm of fear dropped into his gut. He slowed down when he saw the yellow and purple polka dotted tail with the words "Dead Meat," scrawled across it.

Bone heard footsteps running toward him. Quickly, he looked around for an ambush, but it was too late. Alvin Merritt was charging.

Bone screamed.

The oncoming Bull smiled, lowered his shoulder and prepared to collide with the skinny clown and crack his ribs.

Fenimore felt like he was wearing a big red cape that said "Gore me."

The big teen was nearly upon him when Bone unexpectedly fell to the ground and tripped the big fullback. The totally surprised Merritt slammed into the unyielding metal of the lockers as Bone took off running toward the English building.

Stunned by the impact, Alvin staggered for a moment. But the collision was no worse than the time he'd had his bell rung by Jake Simson, the star linebacker at Hudson Military Academy. He quickly recovered and gave chase, but it was too late. Bone had a lead that couldn't be closed. The skinny teenager was not much in a fight, but he could run like a rabbit, especially if he was scared.

The bell rang to begin class as Bone made it to the door of his English class. Before he opened the door to go inside, he turned around and saw Bull standing at the end of the hallway. The big teen pointed at Fenimore and then slammed his fist into a nearby locker. The clanging sent a chill up Bone's spine.

He stepped into the room.

"You're late, Harold," Mr. Kitchens said as he lowered the glasses on his nose and peered over them. "See me after class for your detention slip."

"But Mr. Kitchens, I have a reason for being late."

Kitchens folded his arms. "And what, pray tell, is that?"

Fenimore hesitated and then began his story, "Well, while I was coming to class there was this bright white light and it came down and these little skinny pale dudes with black eyes came out and zapped me with this ray . . ."

The class cracked up. Kitchens raised his

hand to silence them.

"Go ahead."

"So these skinny pale dudes zapped me with a ray and I was frozen."

There was more laughter from the class as Bone continued, "Then they started to examine me, but the bell rang and I guess it disrupted their freeze ray. So I got away, but the close encounter made me late."

Kitchens took off his glasses. "I see. Well, now that you've explained it all to me, I think your little pale friends with the black eyes should have to serve detention with you since they were responsible for making you late. Now please sit down and shut up, Mr. Fenimore."

The class laughed as Bone nodded and went to his chair. As his classmates and the rush that their laughter gave him died down, Bone began to consider the fullback's punched-locker warning.

Why'd I have to hang the tail on the big jerk? Why did I have to do it?

Bone smiled. *Because it was funny, that's why. And funny is what I am. Harold "Funny Bone" Fenimore, Bone for short. Class clown, soon to be punching bag. Oh well, every comic has to suffer before he makes it to the big time.*

His mind turned toward other subjects, specifically Cindy Macleod and the Night Owl Club. Maybe tonight would be the night he would get the courage to ask her to dance.

Yeah, they would fast dance a few songs and then the music would change into a romantic ballad. He would ask her to stay on the floor with him, she would say yes and it would be wonderful as they danced cheek to cheek. And then, and then maybe she would kiss him and they would fall in love . . .

Yeah, and Bull Merritt's gonna forget all about your little joke with the tail, reality whispered in his ear.

Bone shook his head to erase the thought of Merritt's vengeance and turned his attention to Mr. Kitchens who was talking about Herman Melville and the great white whale known as Moby Dick. Fenimore started to say that he knew a man one time who had that disease, but thought better of it. He already had one day's detention and that particular joke would surely get him a week's worth. He kept his mouth shut and let his mind wander back to Cindy Macleod and the Night Owl Club.

The day had gone by quickly as the bell rang for the final period to end. Bone Fenimore walked out of the classroom and immediately looked for Alvin Merritt. Seeing that the coast was clear, Bone took a few steps. A hand reached out and grabbed him. He gasped and shielded himself from the punches he knew were coming.

"What's wrong, Bone?" a girl's voice said. It was Cindy Macleod.

"Oh, uh, hey, Cindy, uh, nothing," Bone said trying to smile while he straightened his posture from cowering to normal. "I was, uh, just imagining Mrs. Ross giving me a Japanese massage with her curly arthritic toes and it scared me."

Cindy laughed. "That's so gross."

Bone nodded. "It's a terrible recurring daydream."

Cindy shook her head. "Where do you come up with that stuff, Bone."

"I dunno. I guess it just oozes from my sick little head."

Cindy smiled and changed the subject. "I wanted to ask you something."

"Oh, really," Bone said wondering what it could be. Maybe she wanted to see if they were going to the Night Owl Club. Maybe she wanted him to take . . .

"Did you get the last homework problem that Mrs. Ross gave us? I was talking to Mary."

Bone tried to maintain his smile. "Oh, uh, yeah, sure." He reached into his folder and found his notes. He handed them to her.

"Thanks." She looked through the notes and found the question. She wrote it into her notebook and gave the notes back to Bone. "I'll see you," Cindy said as she started walking away.

Suddenly, Bone was seized by a momentary

burst of courage. He was going to ask her to go out with him. He raised his finger, "Oh, Cindy, uh, wait."

Cindy stopped. She turned to face Fenimore and he looked straight into her pretty blue eyes. He smiled, lost in her gaze.

"What is it? I have to catch the bus," Cindy said.

Bone snapped out of his daze. "Oh, uh, you, uh, you want to, uh, you didn't get the other problem."

"Which one?"

Bone reached into his folder and pulled out the first sheet of paper he found. He looked at it. "Oh, I'm sorry, that was from yesterday. Sorry."

Cindy shrugged. "It's cool. Now I gotta catch the bus."

"Oh, yeah, okay."

"See ya."

As Cindy walked away, Bone wished that he would've asked her to go out with him. He cursed himself for his lack of guts.

As he started for the bike racks in the parking lot, he reconsidered his actions. Maybe it was for the best. After all, chances were she would've laughed at him and turned him down. Better to play it safe and avoid the humiliation.

As he walked toward the lot, he thought he saw Bull Merritt in his letterman jacket up ahead of him. He turned and went around the building to avoid a possible confrontation.

When he got to the parking lot, he found his bike and unlocked the chain. Climbing aboard, he started to pedal for home. He didn't hear the blue Mustang start its engine, pull out of its parking space, and start to follow him.

Tony Sims lifted his Aunt Ann, into the van. She smiled weakly. The doctor had told them that there was no change in her condition. Tony had lost his mother and father over eight years ago in a terrible car accident. Aunt Ann had become his legal guardian then, and he had been happy with her. Why did he have to lose her, too?

The lung cancer was slowly eating her away. Tony had warned his to aunt to stop smoking, but she didn't stop. Whenever he'd complained to her about it, she'd always told him that it was her body and she could do what she wanted. He guessed she thought, like most smokers do, that cancer only happened to other people. And now they were both paying the price of her actions. She with her life, he with his broken heart.

"Tony, I don't understand it. I should be getting better," Aunt Ann said, then coughed as her son helped her into the seat.

Tony nodded while his heart broke. The doctors had told them that there was little hope of survival for his aunt and yet she still clung to the belief that she would get better.

She coughed with a phlegmy rattle. "Maybe next time."

"Yeah, next time," Tony said.

Tony buckled her seat belt and went around to the driver's side of the car. He climbed in and started the van.

As they drove home, Tony glanced over at his aunt. In one year's time, she had gone from a vibrant outgoing woman to a withered shell waiting to be emptied of life. Her hair was patchy from the chemotherapy, her skin pale and wrinkled. She looked a thousand years old.

"Why so sad, Tony? I told you I'm going to get better, she said.

"Aunt Ann, I want that more than anything, believe me, but the doctors said . . ."

"Doctors! What do they know? There are things much stronger than their puny medicines and treatments."

Tony knew that his aunt was referring to her faith in God. She was a religious woman who attended church at least three times a week, but she was cool about it. She never preached or forced Tony to go with her. In fact, she rarely, if ever, talked about her beliefs. She told Tony that he was old enough to make his own decisions about religion and let it go at that. Her acknowledgment of his independence was one of the things he loved most about his aunt.

God, how he was going to miss her. Tony felt the tears well up in his eyes.

"Please, don't do that," she said as she felt the tears form in her own eyes. "Listen, I know I'm going to get better. I swear it. Any day this thing inside me is going to go into remission, and I will get better." The words sounded hollow coming from the cracked lips of one so close to death.

Tony looked away from his aunt and wiped his eyes with the sleeve of his shirt. "Yeah," he said with little conviction.

Seeing her nephew's depression, Tony's aunt changed the subject. "So how's Bone doing? He hasn't come around lately."

"Oh, he's doing good." Tony said grateful that his aunt had changed the subject. She was so much stronger than he was.

"Does he have a girlfriend yet?"

"Are you kidding?" Tony said grinning. "Bone's too busy playing his jokes. But I think that's because he's so afraid of getting rejected."

Ann nodded.

"I mean he's a funny guy and the kids at school like to watch him crack on people and stuff, but when everybody starts, like, pairing up at a dance or at the club he just kinda gets lost. He has trouble fitting in."

Tony's aunt smiled. "Well, maybe he just hasn't found the right girl."

"Maybe. I just hope that she's a girl who

likes to run."

"What makes you say that?"

"Well, today Bonehead played a joke on one of the meanest dudes in school," Tony said, then began to explain the joke Bone had played on Alvin Merritt.

While Tony told the Tale of the Tail, the subject of that story was riding his bike straight into the jaws of retribution.

As Bone turned the corner of the road leading from school and started down the street leading to his house, he heard the engine of a car rev behind him. He turned and looked straight into the eyes of Bull Merritt. Sitting beside the fullback in the car was Truck Calhoun.

Judging from the look on the Bull's face, Bone expected Merritt to hit him with the car, but the jock just drove past him. Bone sighed with shortlived relief as the broomstick that Truck hurled at him caught in the spokes of the class clown's bike. Immediately, the front wheel stopped spinning and Bone was airborne over the handlebars. He landed in a heap.

The car pulled over and Merritt got out running. He grabbed Bone before he had a chance to get up. Three quick slaps later, Bone's eyes were watery and his cheeks felt like he had a mouthful of wasps.

"Think you're a funny man, huh, Harold," Merritt sneered as he slapped Bone again. "Hanging your little tail on me."

"C'mon, man, it was just a joke," Bone pleaded.

Merritt slapped him again. "I don't like being part of a joke, dipwad."

Bone struggled to break free from the powerful grasp of the football player.

"Hey, Truck, gimme that spray can in the car," Merritt said, jerking his head toward the Mustang.

"Come on, Bull, I won't mess with you anymore," Bone said as he tried to get away from Merritt.

"Damned straight you won't, dipwad."

Bone saw Truck go to the Mustang and pull out a can of paint. The cap looked like it was purple.

"Now we're gonna see who looks good in polka dots," Alvin said laughing.

Bone struggled to break out of the fullback's grip, but he was no match for the strength of the football player.

"Spray him good," Truck said. "I want to see what a purple polka dotted geek looks like."

"Yeah," Merritt said, "so do I." He shoved Bone toward the big lineman. "Hold this dipwad so I can paint him. Maybe he can tell us how it tastes, too."

Bone stumbled and then kicked Truck in the

shin as hard as he could. The big man shouted in surprise as he dropped the paint can and reached for his wounded leg.

"You little dork," Alvin said as he reached for the can of paint. Bone grabbed it and sprayed Merritt right in the face. The jock screamed and put his hands to his face.

Bone tossed the can as far as he could and took off running down the street. Truck took off after him, hobbling from the kick to the shin.

"Truck, get in the car, man," Bull shouted as he ran for the car. The paint hadn't gotten in his eyes. His scream had been one of rage.

Running as fast as he could, Bone cut through a well manicured lawn and ran toward the backyard to escape his pursuers only to be confronted with a chain link fence. He didn't hesitate. He jumped the fence and landed in the backyard.

When he hit the ground, he paused to catch his breath. He heard a bark and turned to his left.

That was when he saw the big doberman and the big doberman saw him . . .

Look for *The Nightmare Club #5, The Room,* on sale in October 1993!

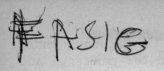

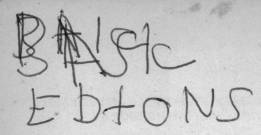

BASIC
EDTONS

***MAYBE YOU SHOULD CHECK
UNDER YOUR BED . . . JUST ONE MORE TIME!
THE HORROR NOVELS OF***

STEPHEN R. GEORGE

WILL SCARE YOU SENSELESS!

prowl parter

BEASTS   (2682-X, $3.95/$4.95)

BRAIN CHILD   (2578-5, $3.95/$4.95)

DARK MIRACLE   (2788-5, $3.95/$4.95)

THE FORGOTTEN   (3415-6, $4.50/$5.50)

GRANDMA'S LITTLE DARLING   (3210-2, $3.95/$4.95)

Coca Coca

*Available wherever paperbacks are sold, or order direct from the
Publisher. Send cover price plus 50¢ per copy for mailing and
handling to Zebra Books, Dept. 4349, 475 Park Avenue South,
New York, N.Y. 10016. Residents of New York and Tennessee
must include sales tax. DO NOT SEND CASH. For a free Zebra/
Pinnacle catalog please write to the above address.*

GOOD N COLD
BY USING LESS
prowd psath.